Rave reviews for award-winning author
Anna DeStefano

"A talented author, who takes a tale and makes it shine... She takes real-life people and tells their stories in a way that will leave your heart aching."
—*LovesRomanceandMore.com*

"DeStefano writes beautifully with a depth of emotion that moves the reader and wraps her in warmth and humor."
—*RomanceBuytheBook.com*

"An author to watch..."
—*ARomanceReview.com*

"Thank you, Ms. DeStefano, for taking real-life situations and developing compelling, entertaining stories that we want to read again and again."
—*Cataromance.com*

"This is what romance should be."
—*Romantic Times BOOKreviews*, Gold Medal review for *The Unknown Daughter*

"A wonderful story...that tugs at your heart and leaves you with a satisfied sigh."
—*New York Times* bestselling author Haywood Smith on *The Prodigal's Return*

"Anna DeStefano's remarkable stories of the healing power of love touch the heart with hope. One of the genre's rising stars."
—Gayle Wilson, two-time RITA® Award-winning author

Dear Reader,

For those of you who've followed my award-winning "Daughter" novels, I'm happy to announce that my Southern-set stories have a new home. *Because of a Boy* is the launch of my ATLANTA HEROES series—where strong Southern men and women fight for love, as fiercely as they battle for everything else in their lives.

Pediatric nurse Kate Rhodes and legal advocate Stephen Creighton are unlikely heroes. Sure, they work hard to help the people their jobs place in their paths. But as they solve others' problems, they avoid dealing with the pasts they don't want to face.

Throw together an injured but determined little boy, an illegal immigrant family on the run from a drug kingpin, hot pursuit from both the INS and drug enforcement officials and a life-or-death medical condition, and Kate and Stephen are at a crossroads. Can they dig deep and work together for the sake of a troubled family, even when the attachment growing between them is more terrifying than the danger closing in? Heroes, after all, might flinch when faced with their deepest fears. But they don't back down—not even from true love.

And for those of you who read *The Perfect Daughter* and asked to see more of Lissa Carter and sheriff's deputy Martin Rhodes's relationship, did you really think I'd leave you hanging? Lissa and Martin's romance continues in *Because of a Boy*.

I love to hear from readers. Please let me know what you think of ATLANTA HEROES at www.annawrites.com. And join the fun and fabulous giveaways at annadestefano.blogspot.com.

Anna

BECAUSE OF A BOY
Anna DeStefano

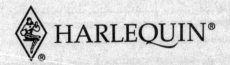

HARLEQUIN®

TORONTO • NEW YORK • LONDON
AMSTERDAM • PARIS • SYDNEY • HAMBURG
STOCKHOLM • ATHENS • TOKYO • MILAN • MADRID
PRAGUE • WARSAW • BUDAPEST • AUCKLAND

ISBN-13: 978-0-373-71449-0
ISBN-10:   0-373-71449-1

BECAUSE OF A BOY

www.eHarlequin.com

Printed in U.S.A.

ABOUT THE AUTHOR

Romantic Times BOOKreviews award-winning author Anna DeStefano volunteers in the fields of grief recovery and crisis care. The rewards of walking with people through life's difficulties are never ending, as are the insights Anna has gained into what's most beautiful about the human spirit. She sees heroes everywhere she looks now. The number one life lesson she's learned? Figure out what someone truly needs, become the one thing no one else could be for that person, and you'll be a hero, too!

Books by Anna DeStefano

HARLEQUIN SUPERROMANCE

For those everywhere who see beyond their lives
and become another's hero.

CHAPTER ONE

"WHAT DO YOU THINK you're doing?" Kate s asked the man standing beside her patient's hospital bed.

The well-dressed stranger stalled in the process of handing the boy something… A miniature sports car. The man raised his deep blue eyes from Dillon, squinting as he locked on to Kate's glare. He gave her a disarming grin.

One she had no trouble resisting.

Her mission as a child had been not falling prey to her brother's Southern charm. It was either that or be in constant trouble for the mischief Martin could so easily talk her in to. Now that she'd reached the wise age of thirty-two, sophisticated stuffed shirts brandishing easy smiles didn't rate a raised eyebrow.

"Visitation for minors is limited to immediate family only," she said in her no-nonsense nurse's voice as the tall, dark-haired man gave Dillon the car.

"But he knows Papa." The ten-year-old, who was usually so withdrawn, flashed a megawatt smile.

The bruises mottling Dillon's right cheek and eye kept Kate from sharing his enthusiasm.

Dillon's joy was palpable whenever his papa was around. The two of them were inseparable at the homeless shelter where Kate volunteered most of her free time away from the hospital. Dillon's unquestioning love for his only parent was what made this situation even harder to accept.

"Look what I got!" he exclaimed, his flawless English colored by a heavy South American inflection.

He held up the plastic Corvette, but Kate could only see the electric green cast that protected his thin arm. His severe ankle sprain had been wrapped to stabilize the joint, and elevated to reduce swelling. Injuries resulting, supposedly, from Dillon's latest *accidental* fall—this time, down the Midtown Shelter's basement stairs.

An accident Manny Digarro had no better explanation for than his only child was more clumsy than other kids his age. Accident-prone. What's a father to do?

"That car rocks, tough guy." She smiled as she walked to the bed.

"It's the one Papa said we couldn't buy when we saw it in the store Monday night."

The same night the little heartbreaker had been rushed to Atlanta Memorial's emergency room—for the third time in two months, Kate had discovered after reading his chart. Though this was the first time he'd been admitted to Pediatrics.

"The boy's father asked me to bring the toy by." The man's small talk didn't distract her from his too-observant gaze. "Seems the nurses at the admissions desk refuse to discuss Dillon's condition when Mr. Digarro calls. He wasn't sure of his welcome if he came himself."

If the hint of judgment in his voice weren't enough, the worry on Dillon's face was all the motivation Kate needed.

"I'll speak with you outside, Mr.…?" She was polite, but he was definitely leaving.

He merely smiled.

Was she supposed to swoon or something? As if she hadn't seen dimples and perfectly straight teeth before!

Screw polite.

She half dragged him toward the hallway.

"Play with your car for a minute, Dillon," she said over her shoulder.

She kicked at the magnetic device that secured the bottom of the door against the wall. Once the door whooshed shut behind them, she released the man's arm, stopping short of wiping her hand on her cartoon-covered scrubs.

Just barely.

"You're *so* out of here." She headed for the nurses' station to page Security, picking up her pace when she heard his footsteps behind her. "I don't know who you are, but—"

He edged around her, putting his body between her and the nearest phone, and bringing her to a skidding halt.

"I'm Stephen Creighton," he announced. "And I represent the innocent man you're so determined to keep away from that child."

"You bet I'm keeping Manny Digarro away from his child!" The nurse who'd rushed Stephen into the hall was furious. "If he does show up here, which I suspect he won't, the staff won't let him anywhere near Dillon."

Stephen didn't have to read her name badge to know she was *Kate Rhodes,* the woman Manny Digarro had warned him about. The homeless shelter volunteer who'd befriended the immigrant family last week, then two days ago had lodged a formal complaint of child abuse with the APD— Atlanta's police department.

"Mr. Digarro's done nothing to deserve this treatment," Stephen insisted, the soul of reason. "You can't separate him from his son. Dillon fell down those stairs, and his father is beside himself worrying about—"

"From the looks of the old fractures on Dillon's X rays, someone should have done more than *separate* your friend from his son years ago."

"Client," Stephen corrected. "Manny Digarro is my client. A good man that I'd be honored to call my friend—regardless of the color of his skin, his ethnic background or his current inability to afford his own home."

Kate's eyes narrowed. If her spine got any stiffer, she'd break in two.

"This isn't about them being homeless, or from another country, or anything other than protecting an abused boy from further harm—by someone who's supposed to love him."

"My client does love his son. Very much. He—"

"Belongs in jail! In addition to his current injuries, Dillon has poorly healed breaks on both arms, his left wrist and ankle. Weeks-old contusions on his chest, to go along with the shiny new ones on his face. And don't get me started on the poor dental hygiene and the vitamin deficiency we suspect is causing his complexion to be three shades lighter than a healthy child's should be."

"Do you find oral hygiene and a healthy glow common among the homeless Nurse Rhodes?"

She crossed her arms. "Once we have the results of the tests Dillon's pediatrician ordered, I'm confident—"

"What tests? Manny hasn't signed consent forms for treatment…."

"In the case of suspected abuse, doctors can sign on the child's behalf. The tests have been run. Once their results are in, not being able to visit Dillon will be the least of your client's concerns. Until then, Manny Digarro should be thankful that restricting his access to the pediatric floor is the only option the other nurses and I have."

The golden-haired beauty's chest rose and fell. The warm green eyes that had smiled down at Dillon sparked with fire.

It was inappropriate, under the circumstances, to find Kate Rhodes's temper tantrum arousing. But that kind of passion was hard to come by in Stephen's world—especially in the defense of another person's well-being. And certainly not in someone so meticulously put together. Stephen would bet tomorrow night's poker stake that Kate rarely let a hair slip out of place, let alone her emotions.

Too bad this wasn't the time or place to push her buttons further, just to see what she'd do next.

Work the case, man.

"You only met the Digarros a week ago," he said, as if reason would work better the second time around. "You didn't see Dillon's accident. Admit it—you don't know for sure what happened, any more than I do."

"Dillon fell, violently, down a flight of stairs. Only his father seems to have witnessed it, just like all the other *accidents*. What else do I need to know?"

"Manny's no more a threat to his child than I am," Stephen assured her. "He's—"

"An abusive bastard who's never going to hurt his son again! Dillon is terrified. He's barely spoken to anyone since he got here."

Stephen blinked and focused past the righteous indignation that he'd label racism or sheer ignorance in someone else. There was genuine fear in Kate's voice.

Most people took one look at an impoverished immigrant like Manny Digarro and saw someone they couldn't trust. Someone they didn't want to be any closer to than they had to be. But Kate Rhodes spent several evenings a week working to help the homeless community. Shielding them from a world too often unconcerned about the well-being of the most needy.

And now she was hell-bent on protecting a child she'd convinced herself had no one else in his corner.

"Manny Digarro's terrified, too," Stephen countered. "He's watched his son have one accident after another, and tried to care for him the best he could, while working countless dead-end jobs to keep them off public assistance. Now he's being told that's not good enough. That Dillon doesn't belong with him. I'm here to make sure someone in this hospital hears my client's side of the story before a terrible mistake is made."

She sized up his Brooks Brothers suit.

"Where did Manny dig you up," she wanted to know, "if he's struggling so badly?"

"At the legal aid center, where he'd heard someone would listen to him, instead of taking one look at his ethnic background and worn-out clothes and figure he was a no-account… 'bastard,' I think you called him, who beats up on his kid to get his jollies."

Her eyes widened. But instead of biting back, she breathed deeply and squared her shoulders.

"Bait me all you want. But my first clue your client was a no-account bastard came while assessing the damage to Dillon's body, not Manny's fashion sense. And you've gotten all the details about Dillon's condition that you're going to. Leave, Mr. Creighton. Or I'll have Security make sure you do."

He stood his ground, soaking in the honesty and integrity rolling off her. Kate Rhodes wasn't on some blind mission to punish an innocent father for socioeconomic circumstances he couldn't control. Instincts that had never let Stephen down screamed that this woman could help his client, if he could only get her to listen.

She started to walk around him. He grabbed her arm. His mistake was instantly obvious.

She didn't jerk away from his touch. She cringed. The agitated breathing that she'd brought under control just seconds before, stopped completely.

Frightened eyes snapped to his face, then dilated.

"Let me go," begged the woman who'd just verbally handed him his ass. "Please, let me—"

Stephen released her, raising his hands to show

he meant no harm, the same way he'd soothe a skittish animal.

She flinched.

"Is everything okay, Kate?" A tall man dressed in blue scrubs, with a stethoscope draped around his neck, glared at Stephen. "What the hell do you think you're doing!"

Making a mess of things.

"Mr. Creighton was just leaving," Kate answered. "Robert, would you call Security to help him find the door."

"No need." Stephen edged away.

He buried his hands in the pockets of his winter-weight trench coat and pulled out one of his business cards from the stack he always carried. He handed it to the doctor, studying the beautiful nurse until she looked up at him.

"I'm sorry I upset you. But please, if you change your mind about helping the Digarros, call my cell any time of the day or night."

He walked toward the elevator, cursing himself for upsetting the woman. She was someone he'd have found himself wanting to know better if he wasn't so certain that she was wrong, dead wrong, about the cause of Dillon Digarro's injuries.

And that her mistake could very easily ruin his client's chances of starting a new life in this country.

ROBERT WAS INTENTIONALLY blocking Kate's view of the lawyer's retreating back, shielding her the way he'd tried to during their marriage. The way she'd refused to let him. He'd always wanted to mean more to her than she could handle—and to save her from things they'd barely talked about.

It wasn't in her nature to want to be saved. It wasn't in Robert Livingston's to back off when he thought someone needed help. Exit one marriage, but thankfully their friendship had survived.

And for the first time, as Kate peered around his tall frame to watch Stephen Creighton disappear into the elevator, she was thankful for Robert's coddling. Because there had been something in the lawyer's earnest expression, in his voice, that made her want to doubt what her own eyes had told her. To believe that an abused child belonged with the man she felt certain had hurt him.

"What was that?" he asked.

"It was nothing," she assured him.

"You okay?" Robert rubbed her arm where Creighton had grabbed it. "Who—"

"He's a lawyer for some legal aid center." She glanced toward Dillon's room. "Manny Digarro sent him."

"The father of your injured kid from the shelter?" Robert was Atlanta Memorial's head neurosurgeon. He worked twenty-hour days, two floors above pediatrics, but hospital gossip spread faster than the common cold. "The man's already lawyered up?"

"Yeah. The police were notified by the E.R. attending, and I filed a report about what I saw at the center. They don't have enough evidence to arrest Manny yet, and we're running more tests to try to figure out how badly Dillon's been hurt. But a fall down stairs couldn't have done all that damage, and there are too many signs of neglect to ignore."

"Sounds like you're doing the right thing. Just don't get too sucked in to it."

"Yeah."

Except she was already in. Deep. X rays didn't lie, no matter how much Dillon seemed to miss his father. And the truth was something Kate had promised herself never to rationalize away again.

She took the business card from Robert, tore it in half and smiled. Tossing it into a nearby trash can, she reassured herself that she'd already put out of her mind how gentle the lawyer had been with her vulnerable patient. How sincere his assurances had sounded.

Only, she'd glanced at the address on the card as she'd ripped it in two. And she'd committed

the name of Creighton's center to memory—
Atlanta Legal Aid.

Damn easygoing, Southern men.

DILLON KEPT HIS EYES squeezed shut.

The grown ups were done arguing in the hall,
but the shaking wouldn't go away.

That nice nurse, Kate, was mad at Papa. Just
like she was mad at the man who'd brought
Dillon the car. And somebody else had been
arguing with them, too.

Dillon wanted to go home.

Not to another shelter, or another city. He
wanted to go back to Colombia with Papa. Except
there were angry, scary people there, too.

Kate had been so nice at the shelter. She'd
taken care of him when he'd been stupid and hurt
himself—again! And she'd been with him almost
all the time at the hospital. He wished she'd come
back, even if she was mad at Papa.

She thought it was Papa's fault that Dillon was
hurt and scared. She was wrong, but she was
worried, and that felt good. There'd never been
anyone else to worry but Papa.

With his good arm, he felt under the blanket.
His fingers brushed the car he'd hidden away.

Kate didn't know it was the first toy Dillon had had since leaving Colombia, or how much of a chance Papa had taken to send it.

We have to be able to move at a moment's notice. We can't risk taking anything that someone's seen us with. That's all they'd need to track us.

Atlanta was the longest they'd stayed anywhere since leaving home. They wore other people's clothes. Dillon's toys were whatever the shelters had. Everything had to be left when they moved. Everything but the clothes they were wearing, and then they got new stuff that wasn't theirs as soon as they arrived at the next place.

He was tired of broken toys, clothes no one else wanted, and all the people he wasn't supposed to talk to. Kids who couldn't be friends. All of it left behind, as soon as something spooked Papa and it was time to move again.

Except now he had his car.

Did that mean they could stop running?

Wait there for me. Try to get better. I'll come get you when it's time, Papa had said as the ambulance men took Dillon away.

When it was time…

Time to run again.

Dillon squeezed the car against his side, missing his papa, missing home—even though home was what Papa was protecting Dillon from the most. Papa was worried about him. The doctors and nurses here were worried. Everyone was worried about everything but what really mattered.

When were the men after his papa going to go away for good? When would it be safe to stay somewhere? To have real friends and real toys, without waiting for it all to disappear?

CHAPTER TWO

"MARTIN STOPPED SMILING a year and a half ago," said the tired voice on the other end of Kate's cell phone. "Nothing I tried here in Oakwood made a difference. Since he's in Atlanta, I just thought maybe you—"

Kate pulled the phone away from her ear and sat in a chair in the pediatric floor break room.

What Lissa Carter thought was no mystery. Neither were the regrets and pointless guilt Kate felt every time she spoke with the other woman.

Lissa's first call from Kate's south-Georgia hometown had been after Kate's brother, Martin, was wounded in the line of duty—a bullet lodged near his spine had left him with only partial feeling below the waist on his right side. Her estranged brother hadn't wanted Kate holding his hand, but his girlfriend, Lissa, had begged her to come home.

But the emotional chasm between Kate and

Martin had been years beyond fixing. Her visit hadn't changed a thing.

Now her brother was in an emotional free fall.

She pulled the silent phone back to her ear.

"He won't see me, Lissa. You know we hadn't talked for years before the shooting. Me being a nurse just adds to the drama now. He moved up here for his own reasons. Reasons that I can assure you have nothing to do with me."

"He's giving up on everything and everyone that used to matter to him. He was pushing too hard in rehab while he was still here. Lord knows what he's doing up there alone. How can you sit by, knowing he's hurting himself?"

Kate resisted the urge to toss the phone across the room. Told herself to calm down.

Lissa hadn't left Martin's bedside for more than a few hours the entire time Kate had been in Oakwood. A year and half later, Martin had moved two hundred miles away, and Lissa was still tenacious.

Kate couldn't help but respect loyalty that rare, that unconditional.   .

"I've tried calling him a dozen times since he transferred to the police academy," Kate explained.

Her brother had hung up on her each time. The last couple of times, he hadn't picked up at all.

"Then stop calling and get your butt over there!" Lissa demanded. "He—"

"Martin's a grown man, and he has every right to make his own decisions, even if they're the wrong ones."

How many times had Kate fought with Robert during their marriage, insisting on the same consideration?

If I want help, I'll ask for it.

I'm not your problem to fix.

"As long as he can take care of himself in that dive of an apartment he's rented—" an apartment Kate had located as soon as she'd gotten his new address from Information "—and can live independently, I have no right to meddle."

"But if you could just get him to let you in." Lissa's voice quavered. "You know, get him to talk about—"

"He doesn't *want* to talk about it! He hasn't wanted to hear anything I have to say since our parents died."

Since she'd insisted on dealing with the truth about their parents' marriage, Martin had accused her of twisting things. Warping every childhood memory they shared.

"Kate—"

"Lissa, I know you love my brother." The other

woman's pain was a bottomless sadness that warred with Kate's determination to stay out of this. "And I know you have Martin's best interest at heart. But sometimes we can take love so far we hurt the people we care about."

Silence.

Kate checked the cell's display to make sure the call was still connected.

"What are you saying?" Lissa asked, tears obvious in her voice.

"If Martin believes you're not what he needs to get better—" Kate laced each difficult word with compassion, the same as she would if she were presenting a risky treatment option to a child's family "—then maybe it's time for you to let go."

"The same way you let go ten years ago?" Lissa demanded.

Kate took a deep breath then said, "I did what I needed to, and Martin knows exactly why I left."

She'd made the right choice. She'd made the only choice she could.

"We would have ended up hating each other if one of us didn't leave, Lissa. And I was the one who couldn't live there and just ignore the truth. If Martin's feeling the same way, and you love him as much as you say you do, then you have to give him his space."

"No WORD YET FROM the hospital?" Neal Cain asked from the doorway of Stephen's office.

The man's customary well-cut suits and crisply ironed shirts didn't soften his dangerous edge. Stephen's boss, the founder of the Atlanta Legal Aid Center, had done five years of hard time— entering the adult penal system as a seventeen-year-old—for a manslaughter conviction he'd copped to, because he'd felt responsible for his best friend's accidental death. His mission now was to make sure the innocents the center defended were safe from the horrors he'd survived.

As soon as Stephen had briefed him on the Digarro situation, Neal had asked to meet the distraught father. Nothing beat the man's instincts with people, and Neal's gut had told him the same thing as Stephen's—Digarro was hiding something, but he wasn't responsible for Dillon's injuries.

Stephen pushed away from the desk. "Nothing official yet." He rubbed the back of his neck, massaging the knots that never completely untied themselves at the end of each day. "I got in to see the kid for a few minutes. He definitely looks roughed up. I can understand the doctor's concern."

"You starting to doubt the father?" Neal gave up lounging against the doorjamb and stepped into the shadows of Stephen's office. It was hours past sunset. Only a desk lamp held back the darkness as Stephen replayed everything he knew about the case, including what he'd seen with his own eyes and as well Kate Rhodes's certainty that Manny Digarro was a threat to the child.

"No," he finally said. "No way is Manny abusing his kid."

"But you don't believe his whole story." Neal sat. Wickedly smart and ruthless, he was responsible for the bulk of their behind-the-scenes work since convicted felons technically couldn't practice law. He was a silent weapon, writing briefs and negotiating deals long before cases could get to trial. He read people better and faster than anyone Stephen had ever met, and he hadn't been wrong about a client yet.

"Digarro never touched his son." Stephen was sure of it. "But that green card he showed us…"

"Yeah," Neal agreed. "It's a forgery,"

And now the Digarro kid was in the system, and the police were focused on the father, while the hospital ran its tests.

"How long do you think we've got?" Stephen asked.

"Before INS comes looking to join the discussion?"

"Before Digarro disappears from Atlanta for good."

Illegal or not, Manny Digarro was fighting for a new start for his son. Stephen could help make it a legal one. There were ways to hold off the INS until the right visas could be obtained, loopholes to wrangle, giving the Digarros time to apply for immigration status and then citizenship.

But deportation was the likeliest outcome if the INS swooped in. Dillon couldn't travel until he was healthy, but his "abusive" father might find himself on the next bus back over the border, then turned over to Colombian authorities.

"Manny's next move depends on what we hear from the hospital," Stephen reasoned. The man had disappeared as soon as he'd handed over the gift for Dillon. "If we're lucky, he'll wait long enough to be cleared of the abuse charges. But we won't have the test results for several days, or so say the nurses answering the phone on the pediatric floor."

A rotating shift of nurses, that so far hadn't included the protective Kate Rhodes.

"And if he's not cleared of the charges?" Neal

asked. "Or if Immigrations becomes an issue? The Digarros are headed for a courtroom either way. You'll work your magic, we'll take our chances, but this one may not be winnable."

"We'll figure something out." Stephen rarely lost. When he did, he sacrificed lives to an unforgiving system. He wasn't giving up on Dillon Digarro's father. "We've still got some time. If we don't hear anything by morning, I'll—"

"How many other cases do you have pending?"

Neal knew how many, of course. He knew what was written on every scrap of paper that circulated the office.

"No more than usual." Stephen shrugged.

"So, you're backed up two weeks out?"

The center's normal caseload would have left the average lawyer struggling beneath mounds of briefs and pending motions, not to mention court appearances that ate entire days at a time.

"I'll handle it." He always did.

"I know. You eat, sleep and breathe this job, the same as I used to." Married and settled now, Neal still beat Stephen into the office most mornings, and he was slaving away most evenings when Stephen headed home. "Look, if you're going to hunker down with the Digarros, consider handing some of the everyday details to the rest of the team. Let Kelly do your research. Give the junior associates a crack at a few of your open cases."

"Yeah, sure," Stephen agreed as Neal stood and walked toward the deserted outer office.

Except Stephen didn't do teams, and they both knew it. Just like he never got sucked too far into a case or let relationships with clients get personal. He stayed in control. Kept things light. He got the job done as quickly and efficiently as possible, and then he moved on.

So why couldn't he get the Digarros off his mind? And why had confronting one feisty nurse that morning so completely thrown him off?

"AREN'T YOU SUPPOSED to be off duty?" a voice asked, intruding on Kate's light doze.

She jerked awake. Her foot slipped off her knee and fortunately planted itself on the floor. Otherwise, she'd have landed on her butt beside the chair she'd dragged next to Dillon's bed.

"Sorry." Her ex stepped farther into the room. He grimaced. "I didn't realize you were sleeping."

"No. It's okay." She wiped her chin, rubbed her eyes, felt her contacts shift threateningly and stopped. Blinking at Robert, she tried to keep the little beasties from rolling behind her eyeballs. "I was just going to hang out for a few minutes. I didn't mean to doze off."

She stood and gently pressed her fingers to her sleeping patient's wrist, checking her watch to track his pulse. Robert had brought the chart in from its holder on the door.

"His vitals were recorded half an hour ago." He leafed through the papers on the clipboard. "Everything looks good."

Kate kept counting. Satisfied, she set Dillon's arm back on the mattress, then turned to find Robert staring at her.

"You stayed in case that lawyer came back, didn't you?" He knew her well enough not to need an answer. "Kate, there are six nurses on every shift. The staff's been alerted to Creighton's involvement with the kid's father. I don't know how he slipped in here in the first place, but it won't happen again. What will your appointing yourself as some kind of bodyguard accomplish? You've been haunting this room ever since the boy was admitted."

"I'm simply following up on a patient's—"

"You have a lot of patients." Robert laid the chart on the end of the bed. "You're off the clock now, but I bet you spent most of your shift in here, leaving the rest of the staff to cover the floor."

"This is pediatrics, not neurology." It had been a frequent argument during their marriage. Robert controlled his O.R. and his staff like a benevolent dictator. He was the master of his domain at Atlanta Memorial, and rightly so. But the pediatric wing was Kate's turf. "One-on-one contact is crucial to a child's recovery."

Robert nodded and picked up Dillon's chart. "He has a broken arm, an ankle sprain and bruised ribs. Relatively minor injuries everywhere else. Regardless of how he got so banged up, or how weak he is in general, neglecting your other patients and your work at the shelter to hold one kid's hand seems a bit excessive, and not just to me."

So, he knew she'd cancelled her volunteer shift at the Midtown Shelter. Normally, it wouldn't matter to Kate how or why her ex had bothered to dig up that fun fact. Except—

"What do you mean, *not just to you?*" she asked.

"Doctors gossip more than nurses do. Isn't that what you always told me?"

"And?" She crossed her arms. Squared off toe-to-toe with the kind but infuriating man she'd shared five years of her life with.

"*And* you have a habit of obsessing about 'pet'

patients. Long before the Digarros, it was someone else, and someone before that. There's always
a reason for you to get more involved than is ap-
propriate, to feel a responsibility for these kids
that goes beyond the boundaries you should be
keeping as their nurse."

"Some people would call that dedication." Just
not Dillon's pediatrician, Dr. *Roger-Every-Nurse-
in-Sight* Floyd, whom she probably shouldn't
have called five times that afternoon. Harassing
the head of pediatrics for test results was over the
top, even for her. But the tests were supposed to
have been ready that morning. The man just
couldn't be bothered to review them.

The last time she'd paged Floyd, his secretary
had threatened to tattle to the head pediatric nurse
if Kate didn't back off. Nurses simply didn't *stalk*
important doctors, who would get around to
looking at test results once they were done with
their weekly golf match with the chief of staff.

The woman had actually used the word *stalk*.

"So Floyd sent you down here to deal with me?"
Kate demanded. Robert had never stooped to
getting involved in hospital politics before. "I'm
simply asking the man to work up the necessary
interest to do his job, so we can document exactly

how badly Dillon's father has been mistreating him."

Robert glanced down at the bed. Dillon was thankfully still sound asleep, but Kate hadn't known that. Openly bashing the boy's father had been unprofessional, and she knew better.

But she'd fed this child food at the shelter. She'd fed his smiling, abusive, no-good father. Her instincts had gone on alert each time. But Manny and Dillon had appeared to be a happy family. On the surface, there had been nothing wrong. Still, she of all people should have known that *on the surface* meant squat when the right kind of evil was festering beneath.

Then she'd found Dillon crumpled in a heap at the bottom of the basement stairs, his father standing over him. Manny hadn't called for help. He'd looked ready to hide. Or run.

He hadn't even come to the hospital with his son.

"Kate?" Robert asked.

She'd moved to the foot of Dillon's bed. She was absently smoothing the blanket over his feet.

Someone had been being abused right under her nose, and she'd shrugged it off. Done nothing.

Again.

"Let's finish this outside." Robert's grip on her arm emphasized that he wasn't asking.

Kate followed, knowing he'd guessed why this case had hit her harder than any of her other *pet* patients'. Why else would he have agreed to handle her for Dr. Floyd? It was sweet in a way. Totally infringing on the freedom he'd refused to accept she needed—even after their divorce—but sweet.

She pulled loose once they were in the hallway.

"Fine, I'll stop bothering *Dr. Important* and wait patiently like a good little nurse." She lifted her hands in surrender. "Your job here is done."

She headed toward the break room and her locker.

"Kate, wait," Robert said.

She turned around.

"I didn't come down here to bust your chops about nagging a man who'd rather be putting on the back nine than piecing a broken kid back together," he said. "Though you might want to rethink how public you make your attitude about senior staff. Not to mention if you want your weakness for abuse victims to become common knowledge."

They seldom discussed her parents. The few times Robert had pried anything out of her, it had been traumatic for them both. There was no way she could feel better about what her father had done to her mother, and there was no way Robert could help.

"Then what *did* you come to say? Lay it on me," she demanded. "I need to get some sleep."

He sighed.

They both knew that no matter how tired she was, she'd stop by the shelter before crawling into bed. Working there was just as much of a compulsion as coddling her patients.

"Roger caught me coming out of surgery." Robert scratched his jaw. "He was bitching about you harassing him—that he didn't have to answer to you and had no intention of taking time out of his day off to be at the beck and call of a nurse. But he did review the test results. He'd planned to phone the on-call pediatrician first thing in the morning."

"In the morning!" Kate gave herself credit for her indignant whisper. Screaming would have been a lot more satisfying. "He couldn't have phoned me or the police with the high points over his two-martini lunch?"

"I know. It's hard to believe, after you've been so pleasant about asking for a favor."

Robert had a point.

Kate hated when that happened.

"I got Roger to tell me what was going on," he added.

And there were times she wanted to hug the guy senseless.

"Thank you!" She squeezed his arm, then his concern registered. "What?"

"They ran a full liver panel." He hesitated, started to speak, then stopped again.

"They wanted to rule out any metabolic reason for why Dillon's so run-down and malnourished," she prompted.

Then Kate lifted a hand to her heart and glanced over her shoulder at the room where a battered child was safely sleeping.

"They won't know for sure until they do a full genetic workup." Robert's voice was gentle. Too gentle. "But it looks like there may be a medical reason for the abundance of badly healed breaks. Diminished bone density. Dillon has been sick for a long time, Kate. And without a proper diagnosis, there was no way his father could have known how to help him."

CHAPTER THREE

A KNOCK ON STEPHEN'S office door caused him to slosh his morning coffee over its rim.

"Ouch!" He sucked his throbbing finger into his mouth. "Damn, Neal. What—"

But when he looked up, it certainly wasn't his boss's silhouette in the doorway.

"Excuse me," Kate Rhodes said.

Stephen took in the soft curves and was grateful he hadn't bothered with the outer office lights. His assistant, Kelly, always took care of them when she rolled in around eight.

"I didn't mean to disturb you," she apologized. "But I was driving by, and I thought I'd stop...."

"Before daybreak?" he mumbled, still gawking like a jackass.

But her voice.

It rushed through him with a zing of both recognition and awareness. As if she belonged in his doorway before dawn. As if there were no more natural place for her.

"You were driving by…." He took a long sip of his coffee, eyeing her over the cup—willing the caffeine to sear into his cells, along with the scalding heat, and fire his brain into functioning.

"I'm getting an early start at the shelter." She didn't appear to have slept any better than he had. "And—"

"And you just naturally assumed the rest of Atlanta works the same god-awful hours as you?"

"I took a chance." She smoothed a hand over her purse's shoulder strap.

The bag was pink. Small. Trendy. Frivolous studs and rhinestones swirled all over it. Why would a no-nonsense character like Nurse Rhodes, who probably lived her life in crisply ironed scrubs or the casual jeans and T-shirt she was wearing beneath her coat this morning, decide to purchase something so feminine and…impractical?

Realizing he was still staring like an idiot, he took another gulp of coffee, set the cup aside and rose to his feet. "Would you like to have a seat?"

"Stephen, have you heard from—" Neal stopped midstep beside their visitor. He automatically began rolling down the cuffs of his dress shirt. His sleeves usually made their way to his elbows approximately five minutes after the man walked through the door each morning. "I'm sorry, I didn't know you—"

"Neal, this is Kate Rhodes, Dillon Digarro's nurse—" Stephen stepped around the desk "—and the volunteer from the homeless shelter who made the 911 call. Ms. Rhodes, meet Neal Cain, the firm's director."

"Ma'am." Neal inclined his head, smiling in that genuine way that Stephen still wasn't accustomed to. Seeing a hardened ex-con like Neal blissfully hitched to a social worker who also happened to be a small-town preacher's daughter took some getting used to.

As did the prospect of Dillon's overprotective nurse hunting Stephen down.

"Mrs. Rhodes?" Neal asked when, moments later, Kate still hadn't spoken.

She was looking back and forth between him and Stephen, as if she were deciding whether to run, hide or fight. The oddest protective instinct had Stephen reaching for her at the same time that she offered her hand to Neal to shake.

"*Ms.,*" she countered, her gaze shifting to Stephen briefly, then returning to his boss. "It's Ms. Rhodes. I'm sorry to intrude so early in the morning, but I…I have news your client needs to be aware of, and I don't know when you'll hear it from the hospital."

She fidgeted with her purse some more. Neal glanced at Stephen for an update.

"No one at the hospital is releasing information about Dillon yet." Stephen had called from his apartment that morning, and again when he'd gotten into the office. "After yesterday, I had the distinct impression you had something to do with that, Ms. Rhodes."

"Yes…" She hugged her arms around herself. "I thought I was doing the right thing for my patient, but…"

"Has something happened?" Stephen resisted the urge to step closer.

Several feet of solid oak flooring seemed like a sensible barrier to keep between them, after her reaction to his touch at the hospital.

"No." Kate eased into one of his guest chairs. Neal did the same. "Dillon's condition hasn't changed."

Neal's encouraging nod was his only reaction.

"I've made a terrible mistake," Kate blurted out. "The test results won't be released until some time this morning, and I have no idea when the police will receive them. But…" She clasped her hands in her lap. "I shouldn't be here…I mean, I'm sure Dr.

Floyd's office will contact Mr. Digarro as soon as possible. But he's a busy doctor, and in case you might speak with your client before… I didn't want Manny to go another hour without hearing the results. I figured he wouldn't want to speak with me, but I thought you'd know how to contact him, and…"

"Contact him about what?" Stephen intruded, encouraged by her rambling, even if he needed another shot of caffeine to help him keep up.

It sounded as if Manny was off the hook. But there was something in Kate's manner that kept Stephen still, waiting for the other shoe to drop.

She looked from him to Neal again, evidently not finding reassurance in either of their gazes. They were lawyers, interviewing a possible witness for whomever might end up prosecuting their client. What had she expected?

She clenched her hands together.

"The test results suggest another possibility for Dillon's symptoms, besides abuse. There's a strong likelihood there's a genetic cause for the bruising and malnourishment—low bone density, throwing off the child's balance. Falls and breaks wouldn't be uncommon." She swallowed. "My suspicions of abuse initiated the police's investigation. I should have waited until the tests were complete, but I didn't. I've caused Mr. Digarro a lot of trouble, and I wanted him to know—" she faced Stephen fully "—I'm sorry."

And she was.

Shadows swirled in her cool, green eyes, along with the unflinching acceptance that she'd been wrong. No excuses. Just the facts, and an honest apology.

Damn.

She'd been overzealous about protecting Dillon, but Kate Rhodes had guts. She was a warrior who fought for what she believed in.

Stephen's kind of warrior.

He'd been raised by passive-aggressive manipulators who wouldn't know how to take care of someone else's needs if their silver-spooned existence depended on it. He'd chosen his path in life, and was now working beside Neal Cain in his brand of ruthless public service, in direct opposition to who his parents had wanted him to become.

It always shocked Stephen to discover in someone else the same determination to make a difference that had driven him since he was a child.

Neal cleared his throat, jerking Stephen out of his thoughts. Kate jumped, too, then looked down to fuss with the clasp of the stylish purse that no longer seemed such an odd fit for her.

The lady was a class act.

"Right." Stephen walked back behind his desk. "So, you're risking trouble with your job, if someone were to find out you're leaking patient records... All so you can tell us that—"

"*Is* someone going to find out?" she challenged.

Stephen waited only a few seconds before shaking his head. "Not from me. All that concerns me in this matter is my client. Notifying Manny might be a bit of a chall—"

His cell phone's ring cut him off. Prepared to send the caller to voice mail, he checked the display. But when he saw his best APD contact's name—the officer he'd asked to keep an eye on the Digarro investigation—he answered.

"Sorry," he said to Kate. "This will only take a minute.... What's up?" he asked into the phone.

"The Digarro kid's gone," Curt Jenkins replied. "APD just got word from the hospital. A nurse checked on him an hour ago. When she brought in his morning meds, he wasn't there. His clothes are gone, too. A janitor on the first floor saw someone who might have matched the father's description carrying a little boy out a side door."

"Anything else?" Stephen made sure his tone didn't change. But Neal shifted forward in his chair.

"Nothing yet," Jenkins replied. "I'm heading over to the hospital to interview staff. Just called the shelter the father was staying at. No one's seen him in days. We'll do some poking around, but I doubt anyone's going to give the family up. The homeless community's pretty tight-knit. I'll let you know if I find out anything more."

"Thanks." Stephen disconnected the call. A negligible shake of his head told Neal they'd go over the details later. "Where were we?"

He returned his attention to the woman who was now standing across from him.

"Something's happened, hasn't it?" Kate's cool gaze dared Stephen to lie to her.

He had a feeling she'd know the second he did.

"How dangerous is this genetic condition you think might be causing Dillon's problems?" he asked.

She blinked.

"If his liver and spleen are as compromised as we suspect, he'll get sicker without treatment. Worst case, he'll need enzyme replacement therapy. Maybe bone marrow transplant, but we can't be sure. Not without ruling out a lot of other things, including cancer. Why?"

"Because Dillon just disappeared, and I haven't been able to reach Manny for nearly twenty-four hours."

"WE'RE ALMOST THERE," Dillon's father promised in Spanish.

Dillon clutched his toy car close. They used English everywhere, except when it was just them. Spanish meant they were alone.

It meant they were safe.

Dillon's arm throbbed and his chest hurt, but so what? He'd ignored it when his papa had carried him down the stairs at the hospital to keep them out of sight. He could ignore it some more.

The cab ride to wherever they were going was taking forever, even though Papa kept saying they were almost there. Dillon's first cab ride. A *real* cab!

But secretly, Dillon wanted his comfortable hospital bed back.

Soft sheets. Nice nurses who smiled and brought him juice. The cab jolted over a bump in the road, and he choked back a groan.

It hurt everywhere, but he and Papa were together again. That's what mattered.

"Thank you for my car," he said. It was too expensive. The cab ride was, too, but he loved them both.

He shifted against the cracked seat.

"You okay?" Papa asked, and Dillon nodded a quick *yes*.

His father was always asking that. He was always worried. They couldn't afford doctors in this country, because they'd left all their money and who they really were behind. But Dillon had had lots of doctors back home.

He might be ten, but he wasn't a baby.

Something was wrong. The tests the American hospital had done felt different. Papa sneaking him from the hospital wasn't right. Spending money on the toy and the cab ride…and just going to a different part of town instead of leaving Atlanta for good—none of it felt right.

They had to keep moving. Dillon wasn't a baby about that most of all. When they stopped moving, Papa was in danger.

His father kissed the top of his head and rubbed the shoulder that Dillon hadn't landed on when he'd tripped down the stairs. The cab jerked to a stop that made Dillon gasp.

"It's going to be okay," Papa promised, the same as always.

Dillon tried hard to believe him.

No one had seen them leaving the hospital. No one would know where they were going next. And Dillon would be more careful. No more accidents. He'd keep moving, no matter how much it hurt.

He was going to get better. He was going to forget about home and the soft sheets at the hospital and Nurse Kate. He was going to be okay, so Papa wouldn't be in danger.

He clutched his new car closer and squeezed his father's fingers tighter, as the cab shot through the next intersection on its way to somewhere new.

MARTIN RHODES reached for the answering machine's delete button. The aluminum crutch propped beneath his right elbow and hand slipped under his weight.

He lurched toward the floor but caught himself on the edge of his kitchen table, jarring it against the wall and sending everything on top scattering. The answering machine hit the tile.

Lissa Carter's endless message kept playing.

"I know you're there, Martin." Months ago, the upset in her normally sunny voice had shifted to something very much like defeat.

Defeat mixed with Lissa's sweet Southern accent made Martin feel like an asshole.

She sounded closer to giving up than he'd ever heard her, which should have been a relief, after six months of him asking her to do just that. Except he hated what this was doing to the strength and confidence that made her so special.

He straightened, his left arm braced against the table, the right against the crutch that was supposed to keep him on his feet, since his right leg still refused to do its share of the work. Easing into a chair, he kicked at the answering machine, dragging it back with his toe. When it was close enough, he bent and picked it up.

Pain screamed down his back. He gritted his teeth against the reminder that he hadn't yet done his daily stretching exercises.

"You've probably been there every time I've called." Lissa sighed. He could hear her girls playing in the background. Something clattered, and he could picture her fussing with dishes at the sink, or cooking something at the stove. "Not picking up the phone won't stop me from calling. Pretending you don't care whether or not someone's in your life might have worked with your sister, but I'm not giving up that easy."

Easy?

Watching Kate walk away ten years ago—
doing nothing to stop her—was the biggest regret
of Martin's life. It had been the catalyst for him
ditching the good-ol'-boy bachelor he'd been,
and ultimately falling for Lissa Carter.

He'd needed something real again. Something
to believe in and hold on to. Smart and funny and
loving, Lissa had been perfect, just as long as his
past stayed neatly tucked away where it belonged.

But flat on his back after the shooting, strapped
to a bed and unable to move and in excruciating
pain, he hadn't been able to keep the shadows
away. And despite the "miraculous" improve-
ments he'd made in rehab, he hadn't been able to
look at Lissa and keep pretending he could be
what she needed. Lissa had to—she *had* to—stop
fighting for them.

A *them* that hadn't really existed in the first
place.

"The girls were asking about you last night,"
she said as the message rambled on. Tears rough-
ened her words. "Callie mentioned you in her
prayers, like she always does. Then she wanted
to know about your legs—if they were getting
better—because she knew how much you liked to
play tag. She was wondering if we could drive up

there and take you to the park to play this
weekend."

Martin stared down at the answering machine,
at the legs it rested against. The small-town gang
shoot-out that had culminated in his injuries had
been a tactical victory for the Oakwood sheriff's
department. Rival gangs in the area were under
control now. The surrounding counties were less
at the mercy of random violence fueled by the
drugs being run up and down the east coast, from
Florida to New York and beyond. A part of
Martin was proud to have been there, to have
most likely saved the life of his best friend—his
chief, Tony Rivers—by taking a bullet while
covering Tony's back. Just not the part that
couldn't feel half of what he was supposed to
from the waist down—the part that still couldn't
be near the amazing woman he loved, and the
ready-made family he'd dreamed of sharing with
her.

"If you want to tell yourself you don't need
us, Martin, then you go on ahead." Lissa didn't
get bitchy when she was angry. She turned an-
noyingly logical and direct. Cool as a spring
breeze.

"Hide there in your new job and lick your
wounds," she baited him. "Try to forget the good

things you're throwing away here, if that's what you need to do. But what about what the rest of us need? I know you're feeling like shit about how you're behaving. Your heart's made of mush, tough guy. You can't keep this up forever, and I have no intention of sugar-coating it for you. The girls miss you. I miss you. Tony's tearing himself up because he couldn't help get through to you. The whole freaking town asks about you everywhere I go. You're needed here, and you're hanging us all out to dry."

She took a deep breath. A sniffle made its way across the line. Then she cleared her throat.

"Fine," she snapped. "Don't answer. Let's see how well you ignore me once I stop playing by your rules. I've left you alone. I've given you time, and waited for you to work through everything. I'm done waiting. Let's see you pretend you don't want me when I'm only a few feet away, instead of halfway across the state!"

She hung up with a clamor.

Damn it!

So he *hadn't* heard wrong the first *three* times he'd played the message.

A few feet away...

Martin's finger hovered over the play button

again, his *mushy* heart clenching at the pain and desperation he'd heard in Lissa's voice.

She couldn't be seriously thinking about coming to Atlanta.

Cursing, he fumbled for the portable phone that had skidded to the far side of the table. His fingers were shaking so badly, he almost dropped the thing. He misdialed her number twice.

Yeah, he was a tough guy, all right.

When the phone rang before he could try again, he thumbed it on without bothering to look at the display. Then he hesitated, not sure if he could actually go through with answering.

Only one person called him at his apartment. Work had his cell number.

He made himself lift the receiver.

"Lissa, honey, you've got to stop this." Her name rolling off his tongue felt so good. "You can't come up here and—"

"Martin, it's me," a different feminine voice said.

This one was clipped yet warm—the paradox a perfect description of the woman it belonged to. The only woman on the planet he was less ready to talk to than Lissa Carter.

"I need your help," his sister said.

Katie.

Someone who—just like him—refused to let herself need anyone anymore.

CHAPTER FOUR

"IT'S MY FAULT they're running, Martin." Kate kept her voice down and her back to the activity bustling around the pediatric floor nurses' station. "I need to know what APD has on the Digarros, so I can help find them. But the officers here aren't telling me anything."

"I work at the academy, Katie," her brother argued, using the nickname he refused to stop calling her, no matter how old she got or how many times she'd said to call her *Kate*. "Even if I was APD, I've only been on the local payroll for a few months. I—"

"You make friends faster than anyone I've ever met." She was being unfair, pressing him this way, after her advice to Lissa to leave the man alone.

But she had to find Dillon. She couldn't be the reason he didn't receive treatment. And since abuse was no longer a factor, the APD officers she'd spoken to didn't seem terribly concerned about making their latest missing person a priority. Stephen Creighton was off somewhere trying to make some headway, but the current consensus seemed to be that Manny had taken his son, and no one in Atlanta was likely to see either of them again.

"You could ask one of your Atlanta buddies—"

"There are no Atlanta buddies!" Martin insisted. "Listen, it's good to hear from you, but I'm not an active-duty officer, and I don't know any in the area well enough to call in a favor. It's almost more than I can manage just to get my ass out of bed and teach every day. It's not like I'm going for a beer with the guys at night."

Of course he wasn't.

He was home shutting out everything he still didn't want to deal with, getting by just fine without her or anyone else in his life. And Kate had left him in peace, respecting his right to make his own choices, so sure she'd been doing what was best—until she'd heard the emptiness in his voice.

"Lissa's been talking about coming to Atlanta," she heard herself say, suddenly ashamed that a woman who'd known Martin for only a fraction

of the time Kate had, was waging a solo battle
to help him.

"Lissa had better keep her butt in Oakwood,
where it belongs. I don't need her coddling me."
Martin sounded desperate not to need anyone.

Kate turned to catch Stephen Creighton talking
with one of the APD officers who was interviewing hospital staff. The lawyer had insisted on
driving her over. He'd seemed impressed with
how hard she was fighting to take care of a kid
she barely knew.

He, of course, couldn't know she'd spent the
past year and a half feeling secretly grateful that her
injured brother didn't expect anything from her.
She closed her eyes against tears she refused to let
fall.

No emotion at work. It was her hard-and-fast
rule.

Not that there was ever much emotion at home,
either, which had done wonders for her marriage.

"You know," she said into the static crackling
across the phone line, "if you ever need anything, I'm just—"

"What?" Martin quipped. "You're just, what?
Planning to help Lissa plan my pity party? You
don't have enough on your plate trying to find
runaway immigrant children with life-threatening

genetic disorders? You're going to take on what's left of me, too?"

She was making things worse for her brother, just as she had for the Digarros. "I shouldn't have bothered you with this. I didn't mean to upset you."

But when she'd realized how much trouble she'd caused, she'd turned to her brother out of instinct.

"It's not you." Martin cleared his throat. "It's good to hear your voice, Katie. It's…it's been a long time."

Too long.

Their parents had only just been buried, after a fatal car accident. She'd been haggling over details with insurance adjusters and an estate lawyer who'd needed an inventory of the things in their parents' house when Martin had stumbled across their mother's diary.

Its pages, covered in Florence Rhodes's shaky handwriting, had revealed the nightmare beneath the veneer of their parents' rocky marriage. A nightmare Kate had known about but had kept secret—much to her parents' relief. Martin, the youngest, had been shielded from a lot of it. The abuse had dwindled to mostly psychological and emotional by the time he was born, but there had still been wounds hidden beneath their mother's smiles and the long-sleeved, high-necked blouses she wore, even on the hottest summer days.

His mother's abuse had been something a grown-up Martin had refused to accept. Or maybe he'd hated Kate for hiding the truth from him for so long. She'd probably never know which.

"Katie?" he asked. "You still there?"

"Ms. Rhodes?" Stephen Creighton appeared at her side, checking his watch.

She'd promised to speak with him about Dillon's condition in more detail once they got to the hospital.

"I have to go," she said to her brother. "I'm sorry."

And she was, about so many things.

"Yeah," Martin said. "Me, too. I hope you find the family you're looking for."

He hung up before she did, her rough-and-tumble brother sounding as close to tears as she was.

"I didn't mean to rush your call." Creighton's harried expression softened when she turned toward him. "Everything all right?"

"Sure." She sniffed back the unshed tears blurring his image.

She'd spent most of the last ten years exiled from the small town and brother she adored.

She'd allowed her crusade for the rights of the homeless and the displaced, and her hypersensitivity to domestic abuse, drive a father to run from the hospital with his seriously ill child. And now she desperately needed a tissue before she fell apart all over a man she'd lost her cool in front of just yesterday.

Life just didn't get any better.

"WHAT DO YOU MEAN the police department's not going to try to find them?" Kate demanded over the bustle of activity surrounding the nurses' station. "A sick little boy is missing."

Stephen weighed his answer, wary of the emotion rippling beneath her words. His gutsy warrior seemed ready to crumble.

His warrior?

Right.

Kate Rhodes wasn't *his* anything.

"It sounds like the authorities aren't going to search for the Digarros anymore," he explained. "At least not at the local level."

"What does that mean?" Even the frown lines on her forehead were adorable.

"I'm not sure," he admitted, but it didn't sound good. "The hospital has assured the APD that Manny's not a threat to his son, just like you said.

It wouldn't take much for officers on the street to keep a look-out for the kid. Except…"

"Except what?"

"Sounds like someone pretty far up the chain of command doesn't want the department on the case any longer."

But why? he wondered. No one from the APD was saying much of anything that made sense, including Curtis Jenkins. Stephen didn't like things that made no sense.

"They have to find Dillon!" Kate pressed. "The doctors won't be certain until a specialist runs further tests, but if it's not Gaucher's disease, there's some other metabolic disorder at work, enlarging Dillon's liver and spleen. I was wrong to accuse Manny without more information, but I wasn't wrong about how much danger his child is in."

"That makes it a medical issue now. APD's been ordered off the investigation." Stephen raised an eyebrow as Kate's frown deepened. "That's probably a good thing."

"How can you say that? Dillon—"

"Is an illegal immigrant." Stephen stepped closer and lowered his voice.

"What?" Kate's fresh scent reached out to him. He breathed her in. His gaze dropped to her lips, then he met her surprised stare and exhaled in an attempt to clear his head.

As if that were going to happen with her still so close.

"I doubt Manny's and Dillon's green cards are worth the paper they're printed on," he explained. "The less the police focus on this family, the better."

"Except Dillon's condition is most likely chronic, and degenerative," she argued. "Mr. Digarro has no idea how important treatment and an accurate diagnosis are, and there's no way he'll voluntarily come back to the hospital now."

"How degenerative? Are you saying the kid's running out of time?"

"The sooner he starts treatment, the less damage his body can do to itself. There are several variations of the disease, not all of them treatable. That's why more tests are needed. Dillon's body isn't storing fat properly. Seizures are possible in the later stages of Gaucher's, as is organ failure, even permanent brain damage. Every major system could be affected if we don't stop whatever's happening."

And she was determined to do just that. Just as determined as she'd been to protect Dillon from his father when she'd thought Manny was the problem—no less committed than Stephen had been to making sure the Digarros got their chance to grab a piece of the American Dream.

Remarkable.

"Where did you come from, lady?"

"YOU DON'T LIKE the APD calling off the investigation any more than I do," Kate challenged Stephen over the rim of her coffee cup.

She had accepted his invitation to stop at a local diner on the way back to his office. Legal, addictive stimulants were her one true vice. And she couldn't shake the feeling that Stephen was worried about more than his client's immigration status.

Instead of responding to her jab, he took a slow sip of his second cup of coffee.

"So," he finally said, "this brother of yours, the ex-cop. He refused to help you look for Dillon and Manny?"

"My brother has more pressing problems than running down information for me." She studied the swirls of cream she was spooning around in her cup, as if they were magic tea leaves eager to impart knowledge. "He's still recovering from the injury that took him out of active duty. I shouldn't have bothered him. Chances are the Digarros have moved to another shelter in town. My contacts in the homeless community might help me locate them. If not, I'll find another way to make this right."

The silence stretched long enough to tempt her to glance up. Stephen was watching her stir. She realized she'd yet to take a sip. That the cup and the coffee inside were both stone cold.

"You're pretty hard on yourself, you know that?" He drained the last of his decaf and signaled the waitress for more. "One minute, you're beating yourself up for trying to protect an innocent kid from abuse. Now, contacting your brother is messing with you, and you're willing to totally disrupt your life to hunt down a family that doesn't want to be found. Is it just the Digarros, or do you figure you're responsible for every bad thing that happens around you?"

Kate was still slack-jawed by the time their server scooted over from the counter. The gum-chewing Amazon—Trina—had had eyes only for Stephen for the last half hour.

Hearing her ex husband's "don't be so hard on yourself" speech coming out of the mouth of a stranger—a stranger she was inexplicably annoyed with for returning the busty Trina's smile—was the last straw.

"I'm out of here." Kate grabbed a few dollars from her purse, dropped them onto the table and fished out her cell phone as she headed for the door.

"Hey." Stephen hustled after her. "What are you doing?"

"Calling a cab." She navigated through her cell's contacts and selected the car service that took her back and forth to the airport when she flew. "I have work to do at the shelter, a long shift at the hospital tomorrow, and a father and son to find."

Stephen's hand covered hers, pressing the phone closed before the call connected.

She'd panicked when he'd touched her yesterday. Her reaction to powerful men she didn't trust was always the same. She'd seen firsthand the kind of damage masculine strength could do to a woman.

Only today, the zing racing up her arm wasn't from fear.

Who knew pleasure could be more terrifying?

"I'll take you back to your car," he said.

"I… I can get back fine on my own."

"Why make things harder for yourself—and take twice as long—when I could have you there in just a few minutes?"

Because *harder* seemed a much wiser choice at the moment.

Stephen's calm, controlled logic unnerved her. His shocking blue eyes focused on her, reading each emotion she couldn't hide—the way he undoubtedly sized up everyone who walked through his office door. It was all too much.

Meanwhile, she was battling the absurd impulse to tell a flirtatious waitress whom Stephen had barely glanced at to back off.

And now Stephen was touching her again, and she was letting him. And enjoying it. A lot.

Oh, stop ogling the lawyer, and get on with it!

"I have a child to find." She tried to pull free. He held fast.

"Good." His slow, Southern smile made her mouth water. "That makes two of us."

"What? Your client's off the hook. You said that *not* looking for him would be the best thing."

"Yes," he began, "except that you're right. The APD being pulled off this case is a red flag. They usually partner with INS. Under normal circumstances, Immigration wouldn't be interfering with local police operations. Something's not adding up, and I have to be sure my client is really in the clear before I can let this go."

Kate could only stare. Stephen's desk had been

overflowing that morning. The man had been buried in work hours before most people poured milk over their Fruit Loops. He had the perfect excuse to be done with the Digarros and move on to his next case. But he had to be sure....

"What..." The word scraped across her dry throat. Where was her cold coffee when she needed it? "What does that have to do with me?"

"I admire people who are willing to go the extra mile to help someone the rest of the world is happy to pass by without a second thought," he said. "Since you're as determined to find the Digarros as I am, it makes sense for us to combine our efforts. When would be a good time tomorrow to start, Kate?"

His question and use of her first name were as much of a shock as the way her skin tingled simply from the thought of seeing him again.

Stephen's connections with the APD would be an asset. For Dillon's sake, she should say yes. But what did she do about the fact that a total stranger was making her wish for things she'd be a fool to pursue?

Reckless things, like trusting him, and having coffee with him again. *Trina-free* coffee. And she admired the fact that he'd been up at six o'clock in the morning, working as hard to help people as she typically was at that hour, and probably not getting paid much more for the privilege.

Which wasn't saying a lot, since her predawn activities were generally volunteer work.

She was in serious danger of liking this man, not to mention needing his sincerely offered help. Neither of which was an option.

"Do whatever you like, Mr. Creighton." She yanked away from his grasp. "Just leave me the hell alone while you're doing it."

CHAPTER FIVE

"WE'VE BEEN THROUGH this before," Robert Livingston assured Martin as he closed the file he'd been leafing through and sat back in his office chair. The neurosurgeon handed over Martin's records. "Your mobility is actually very good, considering the extent of your paralysis."

"Then why can't I get rid of this damn crutch?" Martin shoved the offending item aside, bumping the fishbowl his sister's ex kept on the edge of his desk.

No fish inside, mind you. Just an empty bowl that Katie had most likely tended to while they were still married.

"I understand your frustration," Livingston commiserated. "And I'm happy to keep meeting with you to give you a second opinion on your rehab progress. But this is way out of my field. The best I can tell you is that your specialist's program sounds right on the money."

"My specialist thinks kicking a foam soccer ball around should be the high point of my week. She doesn't get it. I don't care about a damn ball! I want to walk again, without having to hold on to something for dear life."

"The scale of return naturally diminishes the further you get into recovery. Each new task, no matter how small, is a victory. The major milestones are behind you, Martin. You're on your feet and independent. You're back to work and regaining the muscle mass you lost. I've read every scrap of diagnostic paper on your initial injuries, the surgery and everything you've accomplished since. You're already light years beyond the prognosis you were given two weeks post-op."

"Yeah," Martin said, nodding. "I'm a lucky guy."

A walking miracle. But he wasn't back to where he wanted—needed—to be.

"You're impatient," Robert corrected. "And you have unrealistic expectations. In my professional opinion, that's the only reason you've recovered as fully as you have."

He slapped Martin on the shoulder as he stood.

"Just don't be greedy and expect much more?" Martin spat back.

"Not at all." Livingston frowned. It had been

years since the man had been married to Katie, and he and Martin hadn't met until a few months ago. But Robert hadn't flinched when Martin first asked to see him. He was a good guy, even if he didn't have the magic answers Martin wanted. "Keep fighting. But a little perspective on how far you've come wouldn't hurt. You need someone besides me to bounce things off of. I know you and Kate haven't spoken in a long time, but—"

"She moved up here to start her life over when I was being an absolute bastard to her." Martin pushed out of his chair, using the doctor's desk to balance himself as he settled his crutch against his side. "I'm not dumping my problems on my sister now."

"You know, even though we were already divorced when you were shot," the other man said, "I remember when she came back from visiting you in Oakwood. She was torn up. She couldn't help you, and in her mind not being able to help means she's hurting you. Again."

Again.

Silent understanding passed between them. Robert clearly knew enough about the Rhodes family's history to be dangerous.

"If my sister's anything like she used to be," Martin reasoned, "she's already rescuing more people than one human being should try to. She doesn't need me on her radar."

"I think you're exactly what she needs. Maybe *you* can help *her* work through why she spends whatever time she's not in the pediatric wing volunteering at that homeless shelter, putting herself on the line for even more strangers. I never could."

Martin started toward the door. He was grateful for Robert's input, but he wasn't having this conversation.

He'd made Katie feel like their parents' problems, *his* inability to accept them, had been her fault. She'd already been drowning in guilt. He could see that now, looking back at her growing compulsion to exhaust herself helping anyone who'd let her.

Because their mother never would.

"Staying away from you is eating her up." Livingston beat Martin to the door—like *that* was difficult. He opened it, then stood to the side so Martin could pass. "She's still trying to protect you, and she thinks distance from her is what you need. But it's messing Kate up, having you this close and not seeing you. Whatever happened between the two of you in the past—"

"Is the past."

"Not if you can't bring yourselves to trust anyone, not even each another. You're not the only one living with a warped perspective of life, Officer."

Martin made it as far as the hall before he turned around. Robert was right. Some *perspectives* you had to face head-on.

"I'm not an officer anymore," he said as he limped away. "And I'm not what Katie needs to make sense out of her life."

"FULL HOUSE." Neal spread his cards in front of him. "Kings over queens."

"You've got to be kidding me." Curt Jenkins threw down his hand. He looked from his jacks-over-aces full house to Neal's cards. "You're the luckiest bastard I've ever met, man."

Stephen, who'd folded, congratulated himself for losing only his ante. The bidding for this hand had escalated until the majority of both the other men's chips were in play. Their weekly Thursday-night poker match at Neal's place was winding down. About time. Focusing on the cards tonight—focusing on anything all day—had been impossible.

Ever since Kate had stormed away from the diner.

Neal's grin softened the dark edges of his features. "Don't mess with a man looking at a week-long vacation with his bride."

Before roughly a year ago, Neal would never have considered taking a vacation, let alone a wife. But his father's terminal illness had not only reunited father and son after years of estrangement, but had also driven Neal back to the arms of the childhood sweetheart who'd still owned his soul. Then last summer, he'd married Jennifer Gardner.

The couple and Jenn's daughter, Mandy, split their time between his family home in small-town Rivermist and the new midtown-Atlanta condo Neal had purchased to replace the one-room rattrap he'd lived in since he'd left prison. Jenn was arriving sometime tomorrow. And next week Neal and his "girls" were heading for Disney World, where he would be reveling in a cartoon wonderland with the family he'd been so sure he hadn't wanted.

Stephen gathered the cards and shuffled as his boss raked chips across the dining room table. "He's downright unbeatable tonight. Good thing we're only playing for who buys the beer at O'Connel's."

"I'm only buying domestic." Jenkins played

with his anemic stack of chips as Stephen dealt. "You can forget about that imported shit you swill like water, Creighton."

The phone rang.

"I'm out." Neal barely glanced at his cards before tossing them down. He checked his watch and grunted. "Bed time. Finish him off," he said to Stephen as he headed for the kitchen phone, "so I can try some of that Irish ale you keep going on and on about."

Curt scowled as he threw the last of his chips into the center of the table.

Stephen matched his bid and dealt Jenkins the two cards he asked for. Stephen discarded two as well, then replaced them from the deck, and tried not to mourn the damage he could have done to Neal's windfall with the three aces he held in his hand.

"Don't think I've forgotten that you're as crafty as the dark angel in there." Curt downed the last of the beer he'd swiped from Neal's fridge, then tipped the neck of the bottle toward Stephen. "You're more dangerous than he is with that mama's boy smile of yours. No one sees you coming until you're already on top of them. At least Cain's vibe lets a man know to keep an eye on the nearest exit."

Most everyone in Atlanta's legal community had referred to Neal as *Dark Angel* a time or two, though not to his face. When Stephen had hooked up with the center a few years back, he'd been seen as something of a white knight. But he'd been fighting for underdogs a hell of a lot longer than his boss, and he could be twice as mean when one of his clients was threatened.

All Stephen's life his parents had used their money to please themselves, blissfully ignorant of the needs of others who lived right under their noses. Stephen hadn't been able to stomach it, not even as a kid. His crusade to make sure his childhood playmate—the son of the Ecuadorian housekeeper who'd all but raised Stephen—received the same opportunities as he did hadn't been embraced with either open arms or open minds. But once his parents realized he was serious about not going to boarding school unless Frank Benetiz did—once they realized they cared less about the added expense than they did about getting both Stephen and Frank out of their hair—it had been a done deal.

Stephen's first victory at the bargaining table had left him with a taste for more. He wanted to see more good things come into his friend's life, and into the lives of others he'd learned how to help in law school. Strangers he felt he knew better than he ever had his own parents.

Of course, tonight was a different kind of victory. "Never sit down with a player," he warned his friend with a wink as he laid down his hand, "unless you're prepared to get played."

Curt cursed again. "You're full of it, you know that?"

"Yeah." Stephen pulled the last of the man's chips onto his pile. "We all have our special talents."

Yeah, he was cocky and enjoyed more than his share of luck—in both cards and the law. But that enabled him to protect clients until they could stand on their own. He made impossible situations work, then bowed out before he started to care too much about the lives behind the legal briefs.

Something he'd had no problem doing before Manny Digarro, and then Kate Rhodes, had wandered into his office.

He studied his bankrupted friend.

"Are you sure there's no way the department can pursue the Digarros?" he asked. "You and your buddies maybe could do something off the record."

"I'll let you know if I hear anything underground," Jenkins offered. "But according to my captain, any official investigation is off-limits. Someone pretty high up wants the case dropped."

"Who?"

"Beats me, but it doesn't sound local. Eventually, someone's bound to come asking what I know. That should tell us more…."

"But?"

"Have you and Neal considered talking to the INS?"

"What does the INS have to do with any of this?" Stephen busied himself stacking chips.

Curt grimaced. "They were at the hospital yesterday after you and that nurse left. The abuse complaint popped up on their radar. Cooperating with them isn't the best idea I've ever heard, but it sounds like you're running out of options."

"Uh—why would I help the INS hunt the Digarros?"

"The boy needs medical care, right?"

"Yeah. So?"

"I'm just saying there are worse things than sending an illegal family back to wherever they came from."

Stephen inhaled. "Yeah, except I've got this feeling…. There's more to Manny running than just immigration. Why else would someone have called you off the investigation?"

His attention shifted to the downtown skyline outside the floor-to-ceiling window—an urban view that had inspired Neal's wife to choose the high-rise condo over all the others they'd seen. Jenn liked having wide-open space to stare at when she had something on her mind.

Stephen stood and crossed to the window. He could appreciate her point, as he fell into the darkness relieved only by the moon and the pinpoints of light tracing the various buildings rising toward it. *There should be stars out there,* she'd said the first time he'd visited. And there were. You just couldn't see them in town—just as Stephen couldn't yet see what was behind the Digarros' disappearance.

He turned back to his friend. That morning's conversation with Kate had been on his mind all day—and not just because the gorgeous woman had earned even more of his respect by having the guts to tell him off.

"You've taught at the academy, right?" he asked Curt.

"I'm a field training officer. Why?"

"You know anything about a new guy they've just brought in, up from somewhere in South Georgia?"

"Martin Rhodes? Yeah. I hear he was on long-term disability back home, apparently going nuts doing nothing. Didn't want a desk job where he used to work, so he took over teaching defensive tactics up here. One hell of a bruiser, even though he's still limping around on a crutch. Seems like a nice enough guy."

Nice enough to be persuaded to stick his neck out helping his sister hunt down a sick kid?

Didn't Neal keep saying Stephen should use more of what was at his disposal, and not track down every lead himself?

"How hard would it be for a small-town sheriff's department to look into something like an illegal immigrant's history?" Stephen's gaze returned to the blackness beyond the tops of the buildings. "I need something that tells me what the Digarros' next move might be."

Curt's hands were tied. Even if they weren't, with the INS poking around, it wouldn't hurt for Stephen to take his questions someplace farther away. And if Kate and her brother had once been as close as he suspected...

"It's the new millennium," Jenkins replied. "Smaller departments have pretty much the same search capabilities as anyone else. You'd need someone who knows the locals and was motivated enough to contact them for you. You really think this Rhodes guy would do that?"

"It's worth a try."

"You might earn yourself a bit of lead time. But whoever wants the Digarro investigation dropped is bound to flag whatever search is done."

"And wouldn't that be a shame."

Then maybe they'd come looking for Stephen, instead of the other way around.

Stephen liked his cases wrapped up neat and tidy. This one wasn't even close. If the INS wasn't the only federal agency on the Digarros' tail, he needed to know who the other players were.

Kate might not be on best terms with her brother, but Stephen would bet tonight's bar tab that if her brother knew how important Dillon Digarro was to her, he'd find a way to help.

The problem was, Stephen's only viable route to the man was through a woman who didn't want anything to do with him.

"GOD DAMN IT!" Martin Rhodes roared, as he fell ass-backward into the tub. Flailing for a hold on the shower curtain, he felt his right leg twist beneath him.

The curtain rings popped, one after another, the plastic zipping off its rod and wrapping around him as he fell. He landed, hard, and pain shot outward from his hip. His head smacked the built-in soap dish. Pinpricks of light burst behind his eyes.

You need rails on the wall to help you get in and out of your shower, Carmen Lender, his physical therapist, had insisted. *Your balance is still compromised.*

And probably would be permanently, she'd stopped short of saying, but he'd seen the truth in her expression. He might never again be able to do something as simple as taking a shower without some form of assistance.

"God damn it!" he yelled again as he thumped his head against the tile, inflicting more pain on his throbbing skull.

A quick swipe of his hand behind his ear, where his head had struck the soap dish, produced a smear of crimson. Not a lot of blood. No need for stitches. Not that there seemed to be much chance of him de-bathtubbing and dragging himself to the hospital. And no way in hell was he calling paramedics to yank him back to his feet.

He looked down at himself, sprawled, naked. Twisted up in the moldy shower curtain. All because he couldn't stand on his own two feet any better than he'd been able to six months ago, when the "improvement" in his mobility had plateaued.

Plateau, hell!

His recovery was over.

Acceptance sank in. He needed the aids he'd been putting off having installed—*having* installed, when he'd always done his own home improvement before. Even harder to swallow, he needed someone to help him up off his ass before he froze to death. And there was only one person Martin could stand to call when he was this far down—literally. Someone he'd always been able to trust with the truth, even when the truth had been so awful, he'd blamed her for all of it.

The person he'd moved less than ten miles away from when he'd transferred to Atlanta, whose cell number he still had memorized. And she'd gotten his new number, too, somehow.

And what had he done when Katie had called him for a favor? He'd turned his back on her again.

It's messing Kate up, having you this close, and not seeing you....

Martin pushed himself forward, grimacing when his hip wanted nothing to do with grappling for his discarded pants and the cell phone he'd left in one of the pockets. He managed to topple over one of Lissa's ferns, which thrived in the bathroom's steam and the florescent lighting.

But once he had the phone, all he did was stare

at it. How could he do this to his sister? Once she walked back into his apartment, how would either of them escape without being hurt even more?

Especially Katie.

Maybe freezing his ass off wasn't the worst way to spend the night, after all.

"God damn it to hell!"

CHAPTER SIX

"I'LL FINISH CLEANING UP." Kate tied an apron on and turned to tackle the sinkful of dirty dishes.

Even though the shelter used paper products to serve meals, the pots and pans and utensils used to prepare the night's feast had stacked up. So had the list of people who hadn't seen or heard from the Digarros.

Calls were still coming in from everyone she'd spoken to, but nothing promising. Manny hadn't been around for days, and no one had seen a sick little boy in an electric green cast.

She'd even asked those she recognized in tonight's food line. The January temperatures dropped to close to freezing after dark, and since most shelters had a maximum number of nights a person could keep a bed, regulars rotated from one place to another like clockwork. Kate was bound to run across someone who'd seen the Digarros.

"You sure you want to finish all this yourself?" Randall Montgomery looked ready to drop, but he didn't want Kate to have to single-handedly tackle the night's cleanup disaster. "You look like you're running on empty."

"Yeah?" she snickered. She turned on the industrial sink's tap and added dish soap while the water warmed. "Well, you spent the day dashing into flames and protecting people from a three-alarm fire…. You win!"

Randall was a lieutenant in one of Atlanta's fire-and-rescue departments. He'd been on duty that morning, during the downtown apartment blaze every news station in town had broken into scheduled programming to cover. He'd still been in uniform and covered in soot when he'd shown up to help with the shelter's dinner rush. But instead of complaining, he'd grabbed a quick shower, thrown on clothes from the boxes of donations the center made available to everyone and spent the past three hours cooking grilled cheese and heating monstrous cans of tomato soup for total strangers.

"They're not going to show, you know." He grabbed a wire brush and began scouring the stove's cook top. "Not here. Manny's got better sense than that."

Better sense than to trust Kate.

She took the brush away, her glare daring Randall to argue. "Get. I'm staying to clean up, not to stalk a homeless family."

Actually, she was doing both. But she was not about to let a dead-on-his-feet firefighter sacrifice his sleep to babysit her.

"Go home," she insisted. She'd figure out her next move on her own. Somehow, she'd find something, some clue she could follow up on tomorrow.

"You've been on edge all night," Randall pressed. "I hate leaving you like this "

"I'm fine." She shoved her hands into the soapy water. "Get some sleep. You've had an exhausting, superhero day."

He chuckled on his way to grab his gear from the storeroom. "Just make sure someone walks you out when you're done."

The Midtown Shelter was, for hundreds of homeless, an oasis of safety and warmth in the midst of a cold city, but it was also located in the heart of one of the edgier neighborhoods in town. That was kind of the point. Midtown was where community services did the most good.

"I'll walk you out," a familiar voice said. Its husky timber tickled her frazzled nerves, like sensual fingers she wanted to feel everywhere.

The soup pot she'd been scrubbing slipped from her grasp and clunked into the sink, splashing a flood of water in its wake. Her apron fortunately took the brunt of the spill, but she instinctively crossed her arms over her soaked front as she turned.

She glanced at the clock hanging over the doorway above Stephen Creighton's head.

"It's late," she mumbled.

Mumbling was preferable to *Damn, you look hot!*

And Stephen did. Even hotter in jeans and a pullover than he'd been in his ruinously expensive suit that morning.

"Let me help you finish things up." He grabbed a spare apron from the counter and pulled it over his head, then took up where Randall had left off at the stove. "You look ready to drop."

Just what every woman wanted to hear from the sexiest guy she'd ever pitched a fit in front of.

"Is it just me?" Her gaze trailed down what looked like designer jeans, artfully frayed at the hem, to the high-priced sneakers covering the man's feet. "Or is this not your usual Thursday evening hot spot?"

"I begged off poker night early." His smile was a smooth, dangerous thing. "I remembered that this was where Manny and Dillon met you, and wondered if anyone had seen them since yesterday. So I stopped to check the place out."

"Well, no one's seen them, Mr. Creighton." She scrubbed the pot harder, ignoring how good Stephen's aftershave smelled, and trying not to care how unfresh she must be after a long day running around town and several hours of passing out food.

"So I learned. Someone said you'd been asking around, too, and I was pointed back here. I know you don't want my help, but—"

"No, I don't!"

The pot escaped her fingers again, with the same splashy result as before. Only this time, her face was leaning over the sink.

She gasped.

"You okay?" He handed her a towel, blue eyes twinkling.

She wiped away the moisture along with any remaining traces of her makeup.

"Everything all right, Kate?" Randall asked on his way back through the kitchen to where he always parked out front.

She sighed as her friend sized Stephen up—the same way her hulking baby brother always used to, ready to step in and defend her honor if need be.

First her ex, then Creighton, now Randall Montgomery.

Whatever Kate had been doing or saying the past few days that made men think she needed to be rescued, it was time to pull it together.

"I'm fine." She tossed Stephen the towel and grabbed the oversized pot from the soap. "Go to bed," she said over her shoulder to Randall.

She listened to him shuffle away. No way was she looking up again—at him or Stephen. Not until she had her act together.

"I didn't mean to upset you." Even Creighton's voice sounded expensive.

His genteel accent spoke of old, Southern money. It belonged to a man with resources that could accomplish far more, and quicker, than she could searching for the Digarros alone.

"What did you really come here for, *Stephen?*"

Peeking out of the corner of her eye, she watched him turn back to the stove. He folded the towel and set it aside.

"I need to learn more about the Digarros," he began, "without alerting the wrong people that I'm doing it. I need to figure out what direction Manny ran, and…"

He stopped talking and faced her. She realized

she'd just been caught staring at his ass. He met her gaze with a wink.

When she didn't respond—because she was too busy cleaning her pot and ignoring his wink—he stepped closer.

"You said the doctors needed to run more tests," he prompted, "to understand Dillon's condition. He needs treatment as soon as possible, right?"

She nodded. "As soon as Manny realizes it's safe to come back to the hospital, the doctors will—"

"But it's not safe, not for sure, and he knows that."

"Is the INS investigating?" She realized she'd been scrubbing the same spot for five minutes.

She let the pot be and sank onto a nearby stool.

"Maybe," Stephen admitted. "Maybe not. But Manny's not going to take the chance either way. He's more likely to head for some nearby city, or maybe back home to Colombia."

"You think he's already gone?"

"I know I don't have a lot of time to stab in the dark. But Manny may have a contact here I can pinpoint." He waited expectantly. After several seconds, he crossed his arms. "I was wondering if you'd put any more thought into asking your brother for help—maybe through the sheriff's department he worked for wherever he lived before Atlanta."

"I told you, Martin has his own problems to deal with."

"But given the circumstances, you don't think he'd—"

"I spent most of today putting out feelers for Manny, everywhere I could think of. I left my cell number and urgent messages that it's about Dillon. I'm going to do it all over again this weekend, after my double shift at the hospital tomorrow. Don't you think if there was anything I could do besides waiting for Manny to contact me, I would?"

Her cell phone chose that moment to begin a happy dance, ringing and vibrating in her jeans pocket. She nearly dropped the thing as she flipped it open to get to the display. Her excitement evaporated as quickly as it had shot through her.

It wasn't Manny Digarro. It wasn't even a call she was sure she wanted to take, not in front of Stephen. The third ring threatened to make up her mind for her.

The caller would roll to voice mail next.

She turned her back to the ever-watchful attorney and thumbed On.

"Hello?"

"Hey." Her brother's voice was tight.

"Martin, what's wrong?" she asked. "Are you hurt?"

"No, I've just fallen, and…" His gasp broke into a chuckle. "And I can't get up."

Rustling on his end of the line testified to the fact that he was still trying. A sharp expletive followed.

"Stop trying to get up on your own," she chastised. "You'll fall again and break something, if you haven't already. Let me come help you."

Heavy male breathing was the only response she got.

Please, please trust me! she silently prayed.

"I know where your apartment is," she admitted when he didn't say anything.

Of course she knew.

Just like she knew Martin still depended on a specially designed crutch to walk, even though he'd regained significant feeling and mobility in his right leg. She'd met with both his local physical therapist and the one in Oakwood. She knew exactly to the day when her brother had begun growing impatient with his slow progress and had started hampering it, instead of improving further.

But she'd kept her nose out of it, believing that's what he wanted.

Now, he was calling her for help, even if he still didn't want it.

"I'm coming over," she insisted. "Tell me how to get in, so I don't wake your neighbors breaking windows."

Seconds that felt like hours later, her brother let loose another of those chuckles that sounded so familiar, her eyes shimmered with tears.

"My back door's the third from the side parking lot, on the left," he said in a whisper, as if he couldn't believe this was happening any more than she could. "Turn onto Brocket off Spring. The lot'll be your first left. I keep a key buried in the empty flowerpot beside the door, just like Mom…"

"Give me ten minutes." She hung up, fighting the impulse to back out—to call an ambulance and let an EMT handle it.

"Is your brother okay?" Stephen asked.

She flinched, actually dropping the phone this time. She'd forgotten she wasn't alone.

"No." She headed for the storeroom to get her coat and purse. "He's fallen in his apartment."

Stephen was standing in the kitchen doorway when she came back out. He handed her her phone.

"I need to go," she said instead of thanking him.

He didn't budge. "How big a man is your brother?"

"What?"

"I hear he's a pretty big guy. Someone should go with you."

He couldn't be serious.

"Get out of my way, Stephen. You're not following me over there, so you can talk Martin in to helping you find the Digarros—"

"No, I'm not." Stephen sighed, shifting so she could get by. "I'm following you because I'm concerned about what will happen when you try to lift a man twice your size. Think about it. What good are you going to be to your brother or the Digarros if you end up in traction yourself?"

He pushed the swinging door open, leaving the choice to her.

Muscles bulged beneath his long-sleeved knit shirt. Strength she'd already guessed was there. Strength she somehow knew she didn't have to be afraid of.

I'm following you because I'm concerned....

"Martin's place is several miles from here,"

she hedged, "on the other side of I-85. If that's too far for you, I—"

"Not a problem." Stephen fished his own keys from his pocket. "I'll be right behind you."

Sure.

No problem at all.

Except for how grateful she was that he was going with her.

Having Stephen Creighton along shouldn't make it easier for Kate to deal with her brother. But it did.

STEPHEN FOLLOWED Kate's sleek, black Maxima through the nearly deserted, late-night streets, his mind overflowing with all he'd learned about her in the last two days.

She worked grueling hours in unisex scrubs, but in a pair of jeans, her body's curves had the natural strength and grace of a dancer's. And she liked high-fashion accessories, like tonight's purse—black this time, just like her car. She drove a thirty-thousand-dollar luxury car with an engine that purred like it was ready for a motor speedway, but every speck of her free time was consumed by volunteer work in a soup kitchen. She'd dropped everything to help her brother, regardless of their differences. And regardless of her resistance to working with Stephen, she'd trusted him to come along tonight.

You barely gave her a choice!

But she'd trusted him, and something told him trusting people wasn't her thing, any more than it was his.

They turned off of Spring Street onto a side road that fronted several courtyard apartments. The address Kelly had dug up for Kate's place was less than five minutes away. Kate turned into the full parking lot of a neatly kept, older building, and double-parked behind an ancient, rusting truck. Stephen followed suit, blocking in a Toyota he hoped wouldn't need to tunnel out anytime soon.

When he reached Kate, she was staring at the truck as if it were a ghost. He ran a hand over the vintage Ford's tailgate.

"This must be at least forty years old," he said. "Your brother's?"

"My father's." She tucked her hair behind her ear. "Martin never could let it go. He couldn't part with any of my parents' things."

She was already walking toward the building when a thought struck Stephen.

"If your brother can't even get up off the floor

after he's fallen," he asked, "how can he drive that thing?"

She stopped and turned back, surveying the parking lot through the darkness.

"He can't." She headed toward the apartments again. "I'm guessing the van in the handicapped spot is his, too."

The certainty in her voice told Stephen Kate wasn't guessing. The woman no doubt knew every available detail of her brother's life. She went to the back door of the third ground-floor apartment and jiggled the handle. He was eyeing the window set in the top half of the door, wondering how much noise they'd make breaking it so they could flip the inside lock, when she sifted through the sandy soil of a nearby flowerpot and drew out a key.

"Old family tradition." She swallowed, hard. Visibly shaken.

In that moment, Stephen knew pushing to come along had been the right thing to do—damn the Digarro case for tonight.

Kate needed someone there, and not just to help with her brother. The shadows in her eyes had grown deeper. Sadness had vibrated through the word *family* when she'd said it, making Stephen feel ten kinds of protective.

She lifted the key toward the lock, hesitating. Then she sighed and quietly let them in.

"Martin?" she called through the dimness inside, as they both took off their coats.

Stephen followed her through a utility kitchen into a cozy living room that was overfilled with what looked like antique furniture. Only a single lamp glowed beside the leather couch.

As Kate kept walking, he flipped on the overhead lights, illuminating the rest of the space.

"Martin?" she called out anxiously. "Where are you?"

"Down here," a rough voice answered. "In the bathtub."

A sound came from the right, down the hallway. A hallway covered with framed family photos that Kate barely glanced at. Stephen couldn't help but stare.

The smiles on the faces of the people looking back at him seemed so effortless. A family enjoying life. Holidays. Vacations. Birthdays. Kate resembled both her parents. She and what must be Martin hugged each other in frame after frame. Younger. Seemingly inseparable. Happy in every shot, as if they knew exactly how to make each other laugh.

It occurred to Stephen that he'd yet to see Kate smile, let alone laugh.

Her knock on the bathroom door jerked him back to the issue at hand—getting a presumably wet and likely hurt Martin Rhodes on his feet, then leaving him and his sister to work out whatever they needed to.

Stephen joined her at the door.

"Is it okay if we come in?" Kate asked.

"We?" the deep voice countered.

Something that sounded like plastic rustled, followed by a grunt.

"I brought someone to help," she explained. "I wasn't sure I could get you up on my own."

Martin's sigh was loud enough to carry to the hall.

"Sure," he said with exasperation rather than gratitude. "Whatever. Let's get this over with."

Kate's worried glance shifted to Stephen.

"I'll wait here," he offered, not insensitive to the embarrassment the other man must be feeling. "Just let me know what you need."

She gave him a tight smile.

"Give me a minute or two." She slipped inside, leaving him standing there, blown away by her easy acceptance. The unspoken trust it implied.

"Hey," he heard her say to her brother. "Let's see what we can do."

We.

He knew she was talking about her and her brother. That this was about coming to Martin's aid. But the vulnerability she couldn't hide was also making it about Stephen wanting to help Kate get through this without falling apart. To protect her from the emotions he could sense were backing up on her.

Somewhere between here and the shelter, this had become personal.

"Hey, Katie," he heard the other man say.

More rustling followed.

Kate said something too low for Stephen to catch, then cleared her throat.

"You can come on in," she called.

Curt's description was dead-on. Martin Rhodes was a bruiser. Kate had helped him wrestle on a robe, but that was about all she'd be able to do on her own.

Whatever moisture had clung to the man after his shower was long gone. Martin's hair had dried in crazy spikes, and he was shivering.

"We'll get you out of there and get something warm into you." Kate knelt on the mat beside the tub and gently rubbed her brother's arm.

Martin flinched at the touch. His attention cut to Stephen, then back to his sister.

"You help people with stuff like this all the time, right?" he asked.

"Yep. No problem," bluffed the woman whose average patient barely came up to her waist. "I'm going to put my arms around you. You brace yourself on the edge of the tub and lean forward. Let me use my weight to shift you until you can push with your legs, and I'll help you balance."

"I'll slip." Martin shook his head. "My right hip's strained or something. I don't know if it will hold my weight."

"We've got to get you x-rayed." Kate reached toward the robe-covered hip in question.

"Just get me on my feet." Martin shifted away. "I'll stretch things out. Everything will be fine."

"Martin," Kate argued, "I don't think—"

"Don't think!" her brother snapped. "Either help me, or get the hell out."

"It'll work better if I'm in there with you." Stephen grimaced at the anger that flashed across the other man's face. "I can support you while Kate does whatever she needs to."

Martin's reluctant nod propelled Stephen to step into the tub. Kate sighed and waited until he'd positioned himself.

"Okay." She settled into a squat, balanced on her toes.

Martin looked even larger as her delicate arms slid around his wide chest. She could barely lock her hands behind his back. She rested her head on his shoulder, her eyes closing as her brother's body tensed.

"This will only take a second," she promised. "We'll get you on your feet first, then worry about stepping out of the tub. Lean into me. I'll rock backward, then stand. Try to find your balance."

A shaking hand rose to cup Kate's curls. Martin turned her head until she looked up. The big man cursed at the tears in her eyes.

"This isn't going to work," he said. "I'll hurt you."

"I'll balance your weight." Stephen shifted closer.

It couldn't be clearer how much Kate needed her brother to let her help. And that was suddenly what Stephen needed, too.

At Martin's hesitant nod, Kate laid her head back on his shoulder.

"Okay." The supple muscles beneath her T-shirt rippled as she braced herself. "On three. One, two—three!"

The next second seemed to stretch endlessly. She rocked back and lifted at the same time. Martin grunted as he pushed up with his hands and legs. Stephen grabbed his waist, offering whatever stability he could, and prayed they didn't both end up on top of Kate.

Miraculously, everyone found themselves standing. Kate edged away, her hands still reaching toward her brother.

Stephen let go more slowly, watched and waited as Martin braced a forearm on the shower wall.

"Can you step out?" Kate glanced toward Stephen, who nodded in quiet agreement that he had her back—well, her brother's back. "Then you can sit, and we'll see how badly you're hurt."

"Give me a second." Sweat glistened on Martin's forehead. Goose bumps popped up and down his arms. The fingers clenching the robe around him were shaking.

"Let's do this while you still can, man." Stephen wrapped Martin's arm around his shoulder and circled Martin's middle.

"Left leg first," Kate instructed. "You don't want all your weight bearing on that right hip."

Her brother nodded, leaning fully against Stephen for the first time. His entire body was shaking now. He sucked in a breath, and lifted his left leg over the edge of the tub. A deep curse rumbled in his chest. Momentum had him shifting forward too quickly and as he lost his balance.

"I've got you," Stephen said as Kate's hands wrapped around Martin's waist. She pivoted him toward the toilet seat. "We've both got you."

Martin's right shin bumped hard into the edge of the tub on its way over, but they managed to get him seated. He buried his head in his hands, clenching hair the same wheat color as his sister's between his fingers.

"Shit," he said on a pained whisper. "God damn, I didn't think I was ever getting out of there."

"When did you fall?" Kate crouched in front of him, looking as if she desperately wanted to hug him.

She linked her hands together instead.

"I don't know," Martin mumbled. "A half hour ago. Maybe forty-five minutes."

"What!" Kate pulled his hands away from his face. "You waited a half hour before calling anyone!"

Martin didn't respond.

She stood and grabbed the metal device leaning against the wall near the door. The crutch had a hinged section at the top that looked like it was designed to cup the elbow.

"Here." She passed it to her brother. "I'll run you by the hospital, just to be sure you're okay."

"No need." Martin glanced up. "I'm just sore."

"You couldn't stand on your own a minute ago," Kate argued.

"Because I couldn't get to this." Martin used the crutch to push to his feet. The robe settled around him. "It's no big deal."

"It is *too* a big deal," his sister blustered.

"I'm fine."

"You were so fine, you actually called me—*me*—for help." Kate motioned around the bathroom. "You sat on your ass in here all that time, freezing to death, even though you clearly could reach your cell phone. Let me guess. You were debating whether or not sleeping in the tub with a broken hip was preferable to having to see me again!"

"I'm gonna head out," Stephen said.

Brother and sister looked remarkably alike, squared off and both determined to have their way. Blond hair. Green eyes sparking with temper. Stubborn chins lifted. Family stuff was about to bubble up that Stephen had no business witnessing, even if he suspected Kate was setting herself up for an emotional explosion he wished he could spare her.

She'd barely agreed to him coming at all. This wasn't the moment to push things.

"Thank you, Stephen." She extended her hand and shook the one he offered out of habit. A weak smile replaced her frown. Her second smile of the night, even though neither had erased the sadness in her eyes. "I'm glad you were here."

His fingers lingered longer than necessary, as he marveled at the softness of her skin.

"Yeah." Martin watched Stephen slowly release his sister. "Thanks for your help."

"No problem." Stephen turned to leave. "Take care of yourself, man."

Except there *was* a problem.

A big one.

He should be pleased with the night's turn of events. He was gaining Kate's trust. He'd made contact with someone who could possibly get him information on the Digarros. Working the case should always be this easy.

Except the case wasn't on Stephen's mind as he let himself out of the apartment and headed for his car. All he could focus on was how difficult it was for him to leave Kate alone to deal with her brother. How difficult it was for him to leave her, period.

The Digarro case. That should be his concern.

But finding a way to make Kate's serious green eyes smile suddenly seemed far more important.

MARTIN LEANED HEAVILY on his crutch, gritting his teeth. Standing hurt like hell, but that was fine with him. Standing was fan-damn-tabulous. Thank God he hadn't injured anything major in the fall, even if his legs still refused to stop shaking.

"Lissa said you never installed safety aids in the house in Oakwood," his sister said as she watched him fight for control. "Haven't gotten around to them here, either?"

Katie clearly intended to have her say before she left. Well, he'd be damned if that was going to happen in the room where she'd just seen him sprawled on his naked butt.

"So, you have Lissa on speed dial or something?" He forced his legs to move. Okay, so he was not so much walking as shuffling. But he was moving beyond his sister and through the doorway. That's what mattered. "She still planning on taking a field trip up here?"

"I have no idea what Lissa's plans are." Katie followed close behind. Probably had her hands out, in case he stumbled. "She's been calling me off and on. She wants to know why I'm not doing more to help you. I told her I was doing exactly what you wanted me to. And that she should leave you alone if you didn't want her around anymore, either."

He turned in time to see his sister swallow a rush of tears.

He sighed.

"Damn, it's not that I don't want you around," he admitted. "I thought it was better to spare us both this—"

"I'm going to make some coffee." She brushed past him.

"I don't want any damn coffee!"

But she'd already turned the corner toward the kitchen.

"Who said it was for you?" she quipped. "My nerves are shot, so unless you have some whisky around somewhere, caffeine will have to do."

Of course he didn't have any whisky. Neither of them drank, and for the same reason. But she knew he wasn't about to let her get behind the wheel and drive back to her place. Not if she was half as shaky as he still was.

"Fine." He dropped into one of the kitchen chairs. She was already filling the carafe with water. "The coffee's in—"

"The freezer?" She turned toward the fridge. "French roast, right?"

"Right."

And it felt right, having her there.

She spooned dark brown granules into the filter she'd dropped into the coffeemaker. In the light cast by the florescent bulb over the sink, she looked just like their mother had, doing the same task every morning of their childhood. Their father used to drink pots of the stuff. The stronger, the better.

How else was he supposed to burn through his hangovers?

Pain shot through Martin again, generated from his heart this time.

"Who's the suit?" he asked around the lump in his throat.

Katie didn't answer. Just kept fussing with the coffee until she'd turned it on.

She faced him, her expression blank.

"Stephen was wearing jeans." She folded her arms across her chest.

"Yeah. Two-hundred-dollar jeans. Fancy sneakers that cost more than my dress shoes." Martin knew the type. "Doctor or lawyer?"

"Legal advocate. He's representing the father of one of my patients. He was around when you called, so he offered to help."

"Around?"

Martin knew a bit about that kind of *around*. He'd trailed after Lissa Carter for nearly a year, until he'd earned her trust, and she'd given him a chance. That had been only a few days before the shooting.

A few lousy days.

"Stephen stopped by the shelter tonight," Katie explained. "He had some questions about his client."

"And rescuing me from the shower was his idea of a fun way to spend the evening?"

The coffeemaker hissed, filling the room with a rich aroma. Katie opened the cabinet above it and found his mugs as if she'd gotten them there before.

"He was worried I wouldn't be able to lift someone your size." She filled two mugs and brought them to the table. She handed over his coffee, pulled out a chair and joined him.

"Sounds like he's more than just some lawyer if he knows you have a brother who needs help to get up off the floor." Martin took a sip of his coffee. "God, that's good."

"We've spoken a few times." She warmed her hands around her mug. "So have you and Lissa, evidently."

"It's more her talking to my answering

machine, and me listening to the messages. Over and over again."

His sister nodded.

"Lissa's still in love with you." Katie was staring into her mug now. "She's desperate to find some way to help you."

"Helping me isn't her job." Trying to would only hurt her more. "It isn't yours, either, Katie."

"No," his sister argued, "my job has been to watch you shut people out. You haven't let anyone get close since you found Mom's diary. Not even Lissa, not really. And that's fine. Our father was an abusive alcoholic, and your entire family hid it from you. You needed space to deal with that. But now you're hurt, and we're talking about your safety. You've got to snap out of this enough to let someone help you, or you're going to end up permanently disabled." She looked over his shoulder, toward the bathroom. "Or worse."

Martin drained the last of his coffee. He set the mug down hard enough to make his sister jump.

"I'll take care of myself," he said. "Whatever I have to do. I can't keep doing things the way I used to. I get it now, so everyone can get on with their lives and stop worrying."

"Yeah." Katie stood and took their mugs back for a refill even though she didn't need one.

"Except I think Lissa's still seeing you as a *part* of her life. Doesn't seem as though she's giving up on you nearly as easily as I did."

"You didn't give up." He hated the catch in his sister's voice. That the things he'd said out of pain and denial had hurt her. "Don't put this on yourself. You left Oakwood because we both needed you to. And you left me alone here, because *I* needed you to. Don't think I don't know that."

He'd been selfish and hateful, and she'd been tearing at herself about it long enough.

"Thank you," he added, compelled to say it and needing her to believe him.

"For what?" Katie's forehead wrinkled.

His chuckle came out rusty and tired.

"For coming tonight, and bringing the suit who's *just worried* and not scoping you out. For backing me up with Lissa, even though you think I'm wrong. For giving me space, and letting me deny what our father did to our mother long enough to be able to accept some of it."

She refilled his mug and topped hers off, her back to him again. Weighing her options, no doubt. She'd always been so deliberate. Careful. How else could she have kept their parents' secret for so long—and kept her emotions under control, so no one would suspect how much she was hurting.

She returned to the table and set down his coffee. He waited silently as she sat.

"Go ahead," he prompted. "Spit it out, whatever it is."

She deserved her say, and after tonight they might not have another chance. He planned to make sure of it, actually, even if it meant installing support bars on every wall in the apartment, so he'd never put her through this again.

She looked up, tears shimmering in her eyes.

"Katie..." He reached for her. "Don't. I'm sorry I wasn't there for you when you needed to talk things through. It's just I... I couldn't... I couldn't believe that Dad... Even after all the bruises that Mom had explained away. The nasty arguments, and her crying when Dad wasn't around to see it. I—"

Katie was shaking her head. Her hand covered his.

"They're gone," she whispered. She cleared her throat, working to get the next sentence out. "It was a long time ago, and they're gone. *Now* is what's important. What we choose to do with now. We've got to make our lives about what *we* want them to be, Martin. Not about our parents' mistakes."

When he didn't respond, she pushed away

from the table and walked to the sink, which was overflowing with dirty dishes, just like the dishwasher he hadn't turned on last night. She began running water and adding dish soap.

"Stop messing with things in my house!" He struggled to his feet and limped over to her, relying on the crutch more than he had in months. "What I choose to do with my house and my life is my own damn business."

The frying pan she'd started scrubbing clattered into the water. Soap bubbles poofed into the air. She turned the tap off with a vicious snap of her wrist.

"You're not moving on. You moved up here, but you're living with Mom and Dad's furniture. Their pictures. You even kept Dad's truck. You're still stuck in what you want the past to be. When are you going to fight for the future you could still have?"

"I have a home and a new job here. A new life."

"Away from everything that's important to you."

"I'm supporting myself and living independently. That's more than the doctors thought I'd ever do. But taking disability from the Oakwood sheriff's department or working a desk job while my friends put their lives on the line, isn't what I want. Neither is watching the beautiful woman I'd been planning to build a life around settle for half a man!"

He realized he'd shouted the last few words.

His impotence was most likely a psychological problem, or so every physical therapist and doctor had assured him, including Katie's ex-husband. There were no physical reasons for it, at least none that they could find. But regardless of whether he ever got past it, Lissa deserved better.

He was coming all the way back, or he wasn't going back to Oakwood at all.

His sister swiped at the soap bubbles that had landed on her cheek. "If other people are willing to accept what your sacrifice for your job might have taken from you, why are you so determined to quit?"

"I'm not quitting. I'm doing this *my* way, which doesn't include everyone else's 'the sun'll come out tomorrow' bullshit."

"You're cutting your losses." Kate covered his right hand, where it gripped his crutch. "And I understand. I've stayed out of the way. But you scared me tonight. What if you'd broken your neck in that shower, instead of landing on your ass." She squeezed his fingers. "A part of me always thought we'd have time to fix what we've messed up so badly. I thought I could live with waiting until we were both ready. But what if we're never ready?"

"Then we're never ready." He pulled away.

"Is that what you're going to tell Lissa," Katie countered, "when she decides to get up-close-and-personal about being pissed at you?"

He felt panicked at the prospect of actually seeing Lissa again. Weak, useless panic at the thought of her finally accepting that he'd never been the man they'd both thought he was.

He silently limped to the door, yanked it open and waited for his sister to take the hint.

Katie calmly dried her hands on one of their mother's oldest kitchen towels, fished her keys from her purse and collected her coat from the counter.

"Coffee time may be over." She marched toward him, her tears and apologies gone. "But this conversation isn't. I'm as much of an idiot as you are for thinking staying away from each other was the answer."

Her big-sister tone earned her one of his "you're not the boss of me" snickers.

Something inside him shifted as she laughed at his reaction. She'd always had the best laugh.

He'd missed that.

He'd missed her.

"What are you planning to do," he challenged. "Tackle me to the ground and force me to cripple-proof this place? Hold me down, kicking and screaming, while Lissa gives me a piece of her mind?"

"No." She stood on her tiptoes and kissed his cheek. She stepped outside, but hesitated on the tiny strip of cracked concrete that passed for his porch. "But I won't let you forget that I care about you. Not anymore. We're family, Martin. The rest is just crap we're going to have to learn to work around. I have a double shift tomorrow, then I've got to find this kid who went missing from the hospital. But I'm bringing dinner over here Saturday night. I'll make Mom's lasagna. If you're not around, I'll have to leave it at the door for the neighborhood cat. That would be a shame."

Before he could muster his best bratty-brother comeback, she cuddled deeper into her coat and faded into the shadows. Shadows that reminded him that she'd come with someone, and that it was too late even in a nice part of town for her to be leaving alone.

She turned when she realized he was following.

"What are you doing?" She retraced her steps. "Get back inside. You'll trip over something in the dark and do even more damage to your hip."

"I'll go back, just as soon as you're in your car." He held his robe around him. It was freezing outside, and the robe was a size too small. Always had been. But he wore it anyway. Every day. Katie had bought it for him her last Christmas in Oakwood.

"Martin—" She shook her head at his stare, turned on her heel and walked toward the parking lot. "Fine, but be careful. You'd think I didn't walk in and out of the hospital at all hours of the night on my own," she mumbled loudly enough for him to hear." Thank heavens a thirty-two-year-old woman still has big, strong men looking out for her. What would I do, if I actually had to take care of myself here in the big, bad city?"

Despite her fussing, she glanced over her shoulder every few seconds, checking on him, while he watched over her.

It wasn't the warmest moment they'd ever

shared, but by the time she had unlocked her car and was sliding behind the wheel, something about the situation was feeling familiar.

Good.

Right.

"Call me when you get home," he shouted. "So I'll know you got in okay. Either that or I'm following you."

Her growl as she slammed her door and revved the engine earned her his third chuckle of the night. And if his eyes weren't playing tricks on him, there was a smirk on his sister's face, too, as she pulled away.

Ten minutes later, his phone rang.

"I'm home, brat," she announced. "Lasagna, Saturday night. Be there."

She hung up before he could respond.

Always had to have the last word.

Always.

She was done giving him space. Knowing Katie, if he refused to let her in Saturday night, she'd keep bringing over lasagna—his favorite meal—and keep leaving it on the porch, until every stray in the neighborhood was sick of it.

His sister was back in his life, and damn if he wasn't looking forward to seeing her again.

She'd been exhausted, though. Running on

fumes. Coming from volunteering at her latest homeless shelter. And clearly troubled about something besides him.

Probably the missing patient she'd mentioned…twice. The one he'd refused to lift a finger to help find because it would have meant seeing her again. Yet the second he'd called her, she'd dropped everything and rushed over, with *Stephen* in tow as backup.

But Stephen who?

There weren't a lot of legal advocates in town. Martin could understand why—killer hours and crappy money. The man seemed decent enough, but there was something about him that Martin didn't trust.

Creighton was a player. The kind that knew how to use people to get what he wanted. The question was, what did the good lawyer want with Katie?

CHAPTER SEVEN

"INS IS WAITING IN YOUR OFFICE," Neal said over Stephen's cell the next morning. "They seem to think our MIA client might not be as legal as all our carefully filed paperwork says he is."

"No kidding." Stephen was stuck in gridlock, just a few blocks from the office. "A water main break on Courtland has traffic rerouted all over the place. I'll be there as soon as I can."

"Have any luck with *Ms.* Rhodes?" Neal wanted to know.

"Jury's still out." Neither Neal nor Curt would let him live down heading for the shelter instead of the bar last night, despite his insistence that the detour had merely been about the Digarro case. "I may have earned a bit of the nurse's trust."

As if all he saw when he looked at Kate was a nurse.

He was only a block from the hospital. She'd said she'd be working today. And he wasn't going anywhere else, anytime soon. What would it hurt to touch base with her?

"Tell the INS I have a last-minute meeting with a client," he said. "I'll get back to them later today."

"They're going to love that. Have fun with your *client*."

"Yeah, yeah." Stephen hung up on his boss's chuckle.

The man had laughed more in the last year than in the entire time Stephen had known him before, and it only got worse when Jenn was coming to town. Stephen had been hard-pressed to understand the drastic shift in the man's attitude toward life. Work. Everything.

Except, damn if he wasn't smiling himself as he neared the hospital. Because he wasn't just stopping to let Kate know that the pressure to find the Digarros had just kicked up a notch.

He was stopping to see Kate, period.

"HE'S A TIGER IN THE COURTROOM," Marsha Taylor said about Stephen as she and Kate shared a rushed snack of stale muffins and fresh coffee in the staff break room. "Donald says Stephen Creighton's boss doesn't litigate. But Neal Cain has a badass rep for pretrial negotiation. And

Creighton's evidently the last person a prosecutor wants to see across a courtroom. Forget the slick suits and Ivy League manners. Sounds like your lawyer and his boss have an ax to grind with someone, and the legal system's taking the brunt. The more desperate the client, the harder they bust balls."

Marsha's husband was a deputy D.A. on the kind of fast track that left Marsha living the life of a widow for six, sometimes seven, nights a week. Kate had called her last night and casually asked for the skinny on the overzealous but surprisingly attentive Stephen Creighton. Donald Taylor, who struck his own kind of imposing figure inside and outside the courtroom, sounded impressed.

"Did he say how long Stephen's been working in Atlanta?" Kate persisted.

"Since graduating from Emory Law." Marsha wiped cinnamon from the corner of her mouth.

"Expensive." Emory was a six-figure commitment.

"Family money." Marsha broke off the top of another muffin.

She only liked the tops, and Kate preferred the soft, spongy bottoms. Theirs had been a match made in coffee break heaven, ever since they'd pulled their first double shift together.

"That makes sense." Kate sipped her coffee, ignoring her friend's look. The same meaningful stare Marsha had been giving her all morning. "No way does a nonprofit legal advocate make enough to afford that man's clothes."

"And just how good a look have you gotten at those fancy suits of his?"

Kate wadded up a muffin wrapper and tossed it at her friend. "Good enough."

"It might be worth looking a little closer."

Kate shrugged.

She hadn't mentioned how wonderful Stephen had been with Martin last night. How he'd made sure she arrived safely and gotten Martin on his feet without mishap, then faded away so she and her brother could talk. When she hadn't been able to sleep later, her thoughts had drifted back and forth between him and her brother. She'd almost called Stephen's office early that morning—just to thank him again, of course.

Marsha handed over the muffin bottom.

"Rumor is, he has nothing to do with his wealthy family," she continued. "And he spends more of his own money helping his clients after their cases are settled than that center he works at will ever collect in fees. That's all the dirt Donald had. If you want to know more, you're going to have to dig it up yourself."

Kate choked at her friend's suggestive expression.

"What?" Marsha was all innocence. "From what I saw when he was here yesterday, digging could be a whole lot of fun."

"Yeah, like I have tons of time for that." She had a double shift to work, the Atlanta homeless community to hassle and a homemade Italian dinner to shove down her brother's throat tomorrow night. "Fun's going to have to wait a while."

Marsha glanced over Kate's shoulder. "Maybe fun'll come looking for you."

Kate started at the knock on the break room door. She turned to see Stephen peering through the glass inset.

Marsha, ever helpful, motioned him in.

"I'll leave you two alone." She pointed to the counter behind Kate on her way out. "The coffee's over there, counselor."

Stephen turned to watch Marsha go, then pivoted back.

"Hope I didn't interrupt anything." His hands were buried in his trench coat pockets.

"No." Kate stood and swept the crumbs off the table. "Just taking a break."

"Did everything work out with your brother last night?"

"We'll see." She dusted her fingers over the trash can, then rinsed her and Marsha's coffee cups in the sink.

Stephen waited until she looked at him.

"The INS is over at my office right now—" he stared at the tops of his perfectly polished loafers "—looking for information about the Digarros' whereabouts. I thought you should know."

"Oh, God." Kate settled back into her chair. "What have I done?"

Stephen sat beside her.

He hesitated, then settled his hand over hers.

"You haven't done anything," he said, "but worry about a sick kid, just like you seem to worry about everyone else. I shouldn't have been so hard on you the other day. You were doing your job."

"And now the Digarros are on the run, Dillon's not getting the treatment he needs and they may be deported."

His fingers felt good, rubbing against hers. Really good.

"All the INS is doing at the moment is investigating," he hedged.

"But you're pretty sure they're going to find something."

"Yes." His hand squeezed hers. "We're covered at the office. But I don't expect the immigration papers Manny showed us to check out. Or his last known address. The INS will run it all through their computers. If there's a discrepancy, they'll take a harder look. And as long as Manny stays in Atlanta, there's a chance they'll find him."

"I don't see how he could have left yet." Kate tried to breathe through the weight of knowing she'd set this disaster in motion. "Dillon's too weak to travel by bus, even if they had the money. They don't own a car. I'm not even sure they have a place to stay. No one's seen them in any of the public shelters."

Stephen didn't offer empty encouragement or a meaningless "it'll be all right." The fact that he wasn't promising a quick fix made him seem… *safe.* Just like he'd felt safe to her last night, by her side and helping her with Martin.

Stephen's free hand rubbed at the corner of her eye, wiping tears she hadn't known were there.

"We'll find a way to fix this," he promised.

Her breath caught.

We suddenly sounded so right.

"If it's okay with you," he said, "I'd like to talk

to your brother about looking into Manny's past. See if we can figure out who he might have contacted in the city when he realized he needed to hide."

Stephen was asking her if it was okay. According to Donald's "dirt," he wasn't the type of man to ask permission very often.

"Would you leave Martin alone if I asked you to?" What he said next shouldn't mean as much to her as it did.

"It would be a mistake." He smoothed her bangs back, his eyes shutting and slowly opening when she shuddered beneath his touch. "I saw how much you two care about each other. Your brother would help if he knew you were this caught up in finding the Digarros. But, yes, I'll back off and look for some other way, if that's what you need. I'll put a private investigator on it, and see what he can find. Just tell me which way you want us to go."

Kate blinked.

How many times had she told her ex she'd needed to be treated as an equal in their marriage, capable of deciding what was best for her, even if he didn't understand or agree. Robert hadn't been able to do that.

But Stephen, the ace litigator, a master at playing whatever angle served his purposes, was laying his cards on the table and allowing her to choose if he folded or not.

He was saying *us*.

We.

"Kate?" he prompted.

"I…I don't think Martin will agree to help. I'm not even sure if he can…"

"But it's okay with you if I try?"

Kate nodded, only then realizing that Stephen's palm was cupping her cheek.

"I don't know what's wrong with me." She tried to move away.

"It's hard for me, too." His thumb smoothed across her cheekbone.

"What?" she whispered.

"This need I have to trust you." His expression hardened. His gaze dropped to her lips. "I'm not an easy man, Kate."

"No, you're not." She ran her tongue over her bottom lip.

He flinched, and his eyes locked with hers. There was heat there, tempering the hardness.

Anyone could walk in, or walk by and glance through the door's window. But all she could think about was feeling more. Inching closer.

"Do you trust me, Kate?" Stephen asked, doing some inching of his own.

God knew she did. And only He knew why.

"Yeah," she replied, the truth settling deep.

"Yeah," he whispered, a second before his lips pressed against hers.

Get closer.

Feel more.

Make the ache inside stop.

Or make it worse. She didn't care which.

Stephen's tongue grazed her lips, his body tense. He cupped the back of her neck, silently asking permission. When she angled her head, closed her eyes and deepened the kiss, they each groaned.

He took complete control.

There were no other words for the way he devoured her. Then, as her nails bit into his arms, his hands moved down her back, cupped her bottom and slid her closer to the edge of her chair, until her thighs were cradled between his.

She should be protesting. It was too fast. She was out of her mind.

But he was the one to pull away first.

His hands rubbed gentle circles up her arms, leaving her shivering. He gentled his kiss, his chest billowing in and out with the effort it took to back off. Kate clenched his forearms, not ready to let him go, and leaned into his next kiss, pressing for more. She swallowed the low, needy sound he made.

A crash in the hallway sent them springing apart to stare at each other.

Stephen cleared his throat and stood.

"So." He dug his hands into his coat pockets. "Um… Your brother. I'll try to speak with him this afternoon, if it's okay with you."

"He…" Kate stood, too. "I think he's at the academy every weekday. Um—"

The break room door opened. Marsha poked her head in.

"Robert's looking for you." She glanced back and forth between them, as if she could feel the tension still crackling through the room. "I told him you were busy with something important."

"My ex-husband, he's a surgeon here," Kate felt compelled to explain. She shook her head. *As if Stephen cared.* "Yes, it's okay with me if you want to ask Martin for help. But I think you're wasting your time."

"And I think you're underestimating how much he cares for you," Stephen countered. "After what I saw last night—"

"Let me know how it goes," she interrupted.

With a glare, she begged Marsha to keep quiet.

"I'll be in touch." Stephen stepped past Marsha and disappeared into the hall.

"Last night?" Marsha asked.

"It was nothing."

"Doesn't sound like nothing, if the man's already met the brother you haven't said boo to since he moved back to town."

"It's a long story." Kate fished her stethoscope out of her pocket and followed in Stephen's wake.

Marsha kept up.

"So, is it nothing?" she quipped. "Or is it a long story?"

Shaking her head, wishing she knew herself, Kate kept walking.

"THE MEDICINE'S NOT HELPING," Dillon's father said, even though Dillon had been trying to hide how much he hurt.

The medicine Papa's friend at the new shelter had gotten wasn't as good as the hospital's. It made Dillon feel sleepy. That helped. But everything still hurt.

He hadn't been able to swallow the soup the man had brought down to the basement for lunch. Instead of finishing it, Dillon had lain down. If he lay still, it felt less like he had to throw up. And when he closed his eyes, the overhead light didn't hurt his head as much.

Papa patted the car Dillon clutched close, then covered him with another blanket. Papa had been out all day, working—doing whatever job he'd found, so they'd have enough money to run soon. He wasn't sure if he could go out again tomorrow. Someone had been asking for him around town. Asking at all the shelters.

But the manager here was a friend, a friend of a friend from back home. They were safe for a while. He'd keep their secret.

"I'm going to have to take you back to the hospital." Papa rubbed Dillon's shoulder. His eyes were wet.

"No. I'm fine." They couldn't go back. People would be looking for them, and not just the police.

His father nodded. Dillon closed his eyes again.

He wasn't fine.

He'd never been fine, and no one could make him better for good. So Papa had taken his scary job back in Bogotá, to make sure Dillon had his doctors. Then they'd had to run.

He'd said things would be better in America. There'd be no one pounding on the door, demanding to see Papa. No guilt and fear on Papa's face when he had to go see his boss—the man who would kill Papa if they ever went back, or if they were found in Atlanta because Dillon was too sick to run again.

He slid his hand under his pillow and clutched the hospital bracelet they'd cut off last night. The name of the hospital was on it. He had looked it up in the phone book today, when no one was watching. He'd memorized the phone number. Nurse Kate would be there.

She'd worked at the last shelter they'd stayed at, too. He'd found that number and memorized it. Papa would never trust Kate again, but Dillon knew she would help him get better if he called her.

His own eyes were wet now. He squeezed them shut.

Papa had to get out of Atlanta, whatever it took.

CHAPTER EIGHT

"KELLY!" STEPHEN DROPPED the folders he'd been sifting through back to the desk. "The Hastings file, please. Or were you planning to shove it at me through the courthouse window?"

Kelly, blond and leggy and efficient enough for her legal skills to garner more attention than her killer body, calmly glided to his side and handed him the fifth file he hadn't been able to find that afternoon. Almost as if she'd been hoarding the goods, the conniving office diva.

Stephen had admired her spunk from the moment he'd interviewed her. She had the kind of grit any good litigator needed to survive in a courtroom—and she was only a night-school semester short of her bachelor's degree. Then it was on to the law school courses she'd ace, just as she did everything else.

"Keep bellowing at me—" she turned on her heel without breaking eye contact "—and I'm sure I can find somewhere unexpected to shove whatever you want next."

"You love your job," he called after her retreating figure—a petite body nearly every man who came into the office lusted after. One Stephen rarely noticed.

Tall, sleek and athletic women were more to his taste. Kate Rhodes, to be precise.

"I like paying my rent, and I learn something around here from time to time." Kelly rounded her desk. "As long as you keep things interesting, I'll stick around for a while."

"You're great at building team morale." Neal stepped into Stephen's office. He was waiting for Jenn to arrive, then the two of them were taking off.

"Everyone gets their work done and shows back up the next day. Kelly knows the score," he said on a raised voice, just to needle her some more.

All the attorneys they'd hired as the center's casework had begun to stack up valued their jobs and dug deep when needed.

"Working hard isn't all there is to consider." Neal's casual stance was the kind of practiced ease that had lured many a legal opponent off guard. "You can't demand loyalty from people. It takes something more personal than 'do it because I say so' to win trust."

"The staff is paid to be just as loyal as we need them to be," Stephen snapped. Then he sighed as he threw down his pen.

He'd been trying to work for hours, despite the constant flashbacks of having Kate in his arms. He was on edge and distracted, but that was no excuse for being a bastard.

"I'm sorry," he said.

Neal shrugged as he seated himself in the only chair not cluttered with files and papers Kelly hadn't yet processed.

"Keeping things rolling with as little personal stake as possible," he mused. "I saw things pretty much the same way for years. I was as wrong as you are."

Stephen gave up on the Hastings file. "Is making things personal a new litigation tool I'm unaware of?"

"Think of it as a life lesson I'm inclined to save you from learning the hard way."

"You haven't had a problem with the way I've handled things before."

"I don't have a problem with it now. I'm just wondering if curling up with your law books at night is starting to wear a tad thin."

Stephen didn't sleep alone any more often than he wanted to. His level stare said as much, as silence stretched between them.

"When are you talking with the brother?" Neal asked.

"As soon as I finish this brief." Stephen motioned to the open file.

But it was Kate's image that sprang to mind, not Martin's. Stephen could still feel her shuddering in his arms. The memory of every demanding kiss she'd returned that morning had been distracting him all day, making the case more personal by the second.

"Next week's going to be crazy with me out of here," Neal said.

"I enjoy a good challenge."

"Challenge? Like still going full speed ahead on the Digarro case?

"Manny's a client."

"Not since the hospital cleared him of the abuse charges."

"The bogus abuse allegations aren't all he's up against."

"They're all he asked us to represent him for."

"Because he's a terrified parent trying to protect his kid, and he didn't think we'd take the case if we knew he was illegal."

What Stephen wouldn't have given for just one of his parents to have cared that much about him.

A heavy sigh drew his attention across the desk.

"But this case isn't personal?" Neal asked.

"Of course not."

Stephen returned his attention to the Hastings file.

"Good." Neal nodded as he stood. "Then I don't have to worry about you being in over your head while I'm gone."

"Hey, Neal," Stephen said as his boss left.

"Yeah?"

"Keep your cell phone with you, all right?"

"Of course," Neal agreed, understanding more than either one of them would ever discuss. "Delegate whatever you need to. Let me know if that's not enough. And do what you have to do to help the Digarros, and anyone else involved."

"Neal?" Jennifer Gardner popped her head into the outer office. "Ready? Hey, Stephen."

"Have a great trip, you two." Stephen waved as Neal looped his arm through his wife's and ushered her away.

"Take it easy," Neal said over his shoulder.

Stephen's answering smile faded as he had a mental flash of him and Kate Rhodes...arm-in-arm, leaving work early on a Friday, and heading out to do…didn't matter what, as long as they were doing it together.

Where the hell had that come from!

"THERE'S A WOMAN OUT FRONT asking for you." David Weller stepped into the academy's bathroom long enough to relay the message, then ducked back out.

Martin finished washing his hands.

He was actually looking forward to seeing his sister tomorrow night. But he'd counted on having another day to accept their reunion.

He straightened to his full height, grabbed his crutch and pushed into the hallway, walking as normally as possible, his head high, his right leg dead weight but moving with him. His hip was still screaming from last night's slip and slide, but he'd be damned if he'd let Katie see it.

He was willing to welcome back his sister— and their mother's pasta—into his life, but there was no place for her pity.

Except it was a tiny fireball of a blonde waiting in the academy's reception area. She was picking at the wilting ends of the fern no one in the building seemed to care about. Martin had been sneaking it water between classes, or late at night, after everyone else had left and he couldn't stand to go home.

Lissa loved plants. She'd bought him several for his hospital and rehab rooms. He'd found a way to keep them alive those first few months after the shooting. He'd left most everything but his parents' antiques behind when he moved away, except each plant had found its way into the moving van. There was one for every room of his tiny apartment, and then some.

Now he couldn't pass a fern without thinking about Lissa, or keep himself from stopping to touch it, to check if it was getting enough water.

His crutch creaked as he stepped forward. She looked up, the beauty of her smile fading when he didn't return it.

"It's good to see you." She fiddled with a pinched-off piece of fern.

"Why are you doing this?" He glanced to where Weller was manning the reception desk, then motioned Lissa toward the couch no one ever used.

She sat. He walked to a nearby table and settled on its edge, his uncooperative leg stretched before him, the crutch draped across his lap. He usually kept the damn thing as far out of sight as possible. But it was important that neither of them forgot it was there, or what it represented.

"I told you I'd come," Lissa explained.

"Your life is back in Oakwood." He could smell the citrus of her shampoo, the subtle fragrance that always lingered on his clothes after he held her. "Being here is a waste of both our time."

Lissa set the piece of fern aside.

"For someone who gave me the full-court press for as long as you did, you're awfully sure we can't weather our first problem."

"Problem?" The hurt in her voice tempted him to reach for her. He locked his hands together in his lap. "I have to retrofit my apartment to keep from killing myself doing things I shouldn't have to think about doing. I'm fighting to get my mobility back, Lissa, but it may never happen."

"Fighting? Is that what you call ranting at your physical therapist, pushing so hard you're messing with the progress you've already made?" Her chin rose. "Sounds like a temper tantrum to me."

"We may not be able to make love. Ever." He didn't bother checking to see if Weller was listening. "We might never have a normal relationship."

The reality of knowing he couldn't get hard, not even now, with the most beautiful woman in the world sitting within arm's length… He could accept all the rest, but never loving Lissa again…

"Martin—" Shock stole the rest of her sentence.

"Is that what you came up here to get?" he demanded. "You think taking a cripple back home with you will be easier than dealing with a real man after your divorce?"

"I'm sorry to interrupt," a voice intruded from the building's entrance.

Both Martin and Lissa jumped. Lissa pushed to her feet, losing her balance briefly before righting herself.

Fury rolled through Martin. Not at the interruption, but at what he'd just said.

Damn it!

Lissa's ex had left her for his secretary, but she'd rallied and rebuilt her life. She was the strongest, bravest woman Martin had ever met, and he'd just called her a user and a coward.

"I was leaving anyway," she whispered, her head down. But at the door, she turned back. "Be as much of a bastard as you like, Martin Rhodes. Hurt yourself. Hurt me while you're at it. But the only way you're going to get rid of me is to listen to the physical therapist. Then we'll see if we can handle where that leaves us. Until then, I'm going to be an in-your-face reminder of everything you're throwing away."

Martin rose slowly to his feet, but not to try to stop her. His crutch crashed to the floor, his focus riveted on the way his body had tightened in response to the vision Lissa made in a full-on fury.

Her cheeks were flushed, her temper flashing. Blond hair curled maddeningly around her heart-shaped face. She'd looked just as disheveled as she'd looked the one time they'd come close to making love. And his body was reacting now exactly the same way it had then.

He was hard as a rock, straining against the fly of his pants. Friction and shock had him gritting his teeth against the urge to adjust himself in the middle of the reception area.

Good Lord!

When he said nothing, Lissa's shoulders slumped.

"See you around, tough guy." With a glance at Creighton, she turned on the heels of her sexy black boots and walked out.

Martin stepped to follow and stumbled over his fallen crutch. He cursed as he bent to pick up the infernal thing.

"Sorry I interrupted," said Katie's lawyer friend who wasn't a *boyfriend*. Creighton came closer as Martin stood. "I seem to be making a habit of that today. I barged in on your sister at the hospital this morning."

Martin pinned the man with a glare, then headed down the hall. Each step sent a jolt of excitement through his system—originating from the hardened flesh below his waist, and the shock of once again breathing the same air as the woman who'd triggered it.

Lissa.

She refused to believe he didn't need her. His body was clearly taking her side.

Creighton followed him.

"Whatever you want from my sister—" Martin limped into the classroom he had to set up for his next lecture "—you're not going to get it through me."

"Actually, I cleared coming here with Kate first. I didn't want to add to the tension between you." Creighton watched without reaction as Martin set the crutch against the wall and eased into a chair.

"My sister sent you?" Martin asked.

"No." The lawyer leaned against one of the desks. "But she said it was okay if I asked you a few questions."

"About this client you're so determined to find? I figured that was just an angle to get in to her pants."

Creighton grinned.

"Actually, working your sister started out as an angle to get me what I need from you."

"And?"

"And things have changed." A just-the-facts lawyer met Martin's stare. "Kate thinks she's the reason my client and his son are on the run."

"Why would she think that?"

"Because she is, at least in part. My client's son presented all the symptoms of an abused child. He was hurt at her shelter, and Kate alerted the police about the father's likely responsibility for his injuries. There was no abuse, but now my client's citizenship is in question. Maybe more. The father ran with the boy, the INS is on their tail and APD has been called off by someone who doesn't want to openly play their hand yet. Meanwhile, a missing kid isn't getting the medical care he needs."

"And you're blaming Katie?"

"No, but your sister's feeling guilty as hell, all the same. I'd very much like to help her let herself off the hook. To do that, I need information that my local contacts can't get me. Fast." The lawyer nodded Martin's way. "Do you have anyone back in that sheriff's department you left that could help me?"

"I NEED A ROOMMATE," announced the small-town beauty waiting outside Kate's condominium later that evening.

Lissa Carter was perched on the first of two suitcases. Her expression hinted strongly of mischief and desperation.

Kate sighed and handed the woman the overflowing grocery bags she'd lugged from her car. She unlocked the door, reclaimed the bags and motioned for the love of her brother's life to precede her inside.

"Does Martin know you're here?" she asked, not that she didn't welcome the diversion.

There was still no news on the Digarros. No word from Stephen since that morning. She'd just rolled off a double shift at the hospital, and she'd known she wouldn't be able to sleep. So she'd planned to get a jump-start on the lasagna for tomorrow night's dinner.

"I saw Martin earlier today." Lissa picked up her luggage and trudged to the couch to sit. "I might have forgotten to mention that I planned to mooch a room from you."

"You're not mooching." Kate sat beside her. "You're worried about someone I care for deeply. You can stay as long as you want."

Kate deserved the other woman's shocked expression.

It felt good to finally be doing the right thing.

Martin didn't want the people who loved him to keep fighting for him, but it was what he needed. Sweet, gentle Lissa Carter had accepted that from the start. Kate envied the woman her ability to fearlessly follow her heart.

After only a few meaningless kisses, Kate was questioning if she could handle seeing Stephen Creighton again.

Suddenly, a plan to harness some of Lissa's tough love began formulating in Kate's mind.

She returned to where she'd set down the shopping bags. "How good are you at infiltrating enemy territory—" she pulled out a box of lasagna noodles and shook it "—while wielding homemade Italian casserole?"

CHAPTER NINE

"LOOKS LIKE YOUR MAN has good reason to stay one step ahead of the authorities," Martin said over Stephen's cell Saturday morning.

"How bad is it?" Stephen pushed himself out of bed and padded to the kitchen to kick-start the coffeemaker a full hour before he'd programmed it to fire up.

"From what little I've heard from my DEA contacts, returning to Colombia would be a death sentence."

"DEA? So, it's drugs." Stephen double-checked the stove's digital clock, calculating how early would be too early to call Neal on the first day of his vacation. "Manny Digarro doesn't seem the type."

"Word is, *Manuel* worked for some drug lord living on a mountain outside Bogotá. He's some financial wizard with accounting and investments and did the books for the head guy himself. I've got nothing yet on whether or not your client's last name's legit, by the way. He dropped out of sight something like a year ago. There's a price on his head. No clear read on why."

Stephen sighed. "So his kid being admitted to the hospital, and the APD nosing around asking questions put him on more than the INS radar?"

"There's no way to tell for sure, but it sounds like there were some rumblings on the street before my guy started inquiring. Someone's been tailing your client for a while."

"You have a contact high enough in the DEA to get this kind of information overnight?"

"It's not my contact, but it's solid. My chief from back home put out a few feelers. I doubt the APD or INS is going to get wind of it right away, but they're not who you should be worried about. In fact, you might *want* them involved by the time this all plays out."

Stephen's opinion of Kate's brother notched up even higher. It hadn't sounded like Martin wanted anything more to do with "back home" than Manny—Manuel—Digarro did. Except Kate had needed him to call in an old marker. And so he had.

Martin's last statement registered.

"You're thinking the Digarros might have to

turn themselves in for their own protection," Stephen summed up.

"The Vargas cartel Digarro worked for has strong ties in the States. People don't *leave* an organization like that, not people in as deep as it seems your guy was. They're going to want him—or something he took—back. Or they're going to want him dead. Neither one sounds like a good situation for a sick kid."

"Does Kate know any of this yet?"

She'd be even more desperate to find the family now.

"She's bringing dinner over tonight." What Martin didn't quite achieve in enthusiasm for the visit, he made up for by sounding worried about his sister. "It'll keep until then, unless you're going to speak with her first."

"I hadn't planned to." Stephen had a buttload of work piling up at the office, as well as trying to find a precedent that would give the Digarros some protection under current immigration statutes. Not to mention that he needed more time to figure out what his and Kate's kiss had meant... or not meant. "What are you going to suggest she do?"

There was only silence on the other end of the phone.

"We'll have to be careful how we approach the man," Rhodes finally said.

"We?"

"*You* have to talk the guy in. Find him some place safe to perch, so Kate can get his kid the help he needs, and the father can consider his options. Then you're going to have to do some of that fancy legal shit I hear you're so good at, and get the INS or whoever else in the mood to deal. You got somewhere to take the family once you find them?"

"I have a few contacts." Stephen added Curt Jenkins to his call list. For someone who didn't do teamwork, Stephen was amassing quite a posse. "I should be able to work something out. Are you in this for the duration?"

"I'm not sure how much good I'll do you, but, yeah, I'm in."

Kate's brother sounded committed, the way Stephen suspected the man had been as a sheriff's deputy. As determined as his sister was when Kate had her sights set on something she wanted.

Stephen closed his eyes against the memory of her reaching for him.

Of *him* being what she'd wanted.

"You want to tell Katie, instead of me?" Martin asked.

It was a leading question if Stephen had ever heard one. The man wanted to know just how much Stephen already figured in his sister's life. Or maybe how much Stephen *wanted* to figure.

Was he focused on what Kate needed, or was he still working his own agenda?

"She needs to hear this from you," Stephen said without hesitation.

He wanted to be there, to help her process the latest round of bad news. And he would be, he realized. Nothing short of her asking him to leave could keep him away tonight. But she had to work out as much as she could with her brother, too.

She needed to know what Martin had done for her. What he was still willing to do for her.

"It'll mean a lot to Kate, to know you're helping out," Stephen added.

"You know, you're not exactly what I expected," Martin admitted.

Stephen shook his head.

Turned out, since meeting Kate, *he* wasn't anything close to what he'd expected, either.

"WE'LL MAKE THIS WORK," Kate promised the woman she suspected might one day become her sister-in-law—if what they were about to do didn't end Lissa's chances once and for all.

"This is dirty pool," Lissa countered as they walked from the parking lot to Martin's apartment. "Even if I am grateful you're letting me tag along."

"I was always better at pool than my brother," Kate assured her.

Because she'd cheated and moved the balls while Martin had pretended not to look. Technically that meant she wasn't to be trusted, and he'd let her win. But the point was she'd won. Martin was one of the most competitive men she'd ever met, but he had a soul-deep soft spot buried under all that macho.

Lissa hefted the bag filled with garlic bread, salad mix and a bottle of wine they'd thrown in for good measure.

"Here goes nothing." She stepped around Kate to knock on the door. "Eight ball in the corner pocket."

Kate was still chuckling when the door swung open.

Martin swallowed his welcoming smile at the sight of them. Lissa shoved the groceries at him and breezed inside.

"You should open the wine and let it breathe for a while," she said. She was already fiddling with the dials on the stove by the time Kate stepped inside. "Do you have any pans for the garlic bread?"

"Do I have pans!" Martin shadowed Lissa, his limp barely discernable. He dumped the bags on the counter. "No, I've been boiling water in my bare hands!"

Lissa started opening drawers, searching for something.

"Ah!" She wielded a box of aluminum foil like a sword against Martin's chest. "Perfect. Where do you keep your knives? I need something to spread garlic butter."

"You don't need a knife." Martin slapped the foil down beside the food. "You won't be staying long enough to use it."

But Lissa had found the silverware drawer, then the knife. She scooted back to the bags for the bread and butter.

"Garlic powder?" she asked sweetly.

Martin gulped, then rounded on Kate.

"If this is your idea of some kind of—"

"*This* is dinner," Kate affirmed.

"This is an ambush."

"Nope, it's lasagna." She handed over the baking dish. "Three-fifty for thirty minutes or so, and it should be bubbling and ready."

"Katie—" He set the pasta aside and grabbed her elbow. "This isn't right, and you know it."

"Sometimes, right doesn't get the job done, baby brother."

Until yesterday's kiss with Stephen, *alone* had always seemed right to Kate, even when she'd been married to Robert. And even with Stephen—especially with someone who made her feel as amazing as he did—she still wasn't sure she could belong.

She didn't want that kind of *right* for Martin.

"I need to talk to you." He steered her toward the living room. "It's—"

"We'll talk." She dug in her heels. "I'm glad you want to. But tonight, you and Lissa—"

"It's about Manny and Dillon Digarro." His grip gentled. "Stephen Creighton asked me to look in to a few things. I ran some details by him this morning. He thought you'd be more comfortable hearing them from me. He thought—"

"That it would be a good thing for us to talk it through together." Just as he'd given them time Thursday night, after he'd made sure she'd survived extracting her two-hundred-plus-pound brother from the bath.

That's why he hadn't called all day, while she'd been assuming he was regretting what had happened at the hospital.

"He really is a good guy, isn't he?" she asked the universe in general.

Martin shrugged. His grim expression registered.

"How much trouble are the Digarros in?"

"They were in trouble a long time before that kid got hurt at your shelter," her brother responded.

"And…" When he hesitated, she pointed a sisterly finger. "Don't sugarcoat things for me, Martin. Tell me what you found."

Lissa shut the stove after putting the casserole in.

"Is something wrong?" she asked.

Martin shook his head and patted Kate's arm.

"We can go over it after dinner," he offered, "if—"

"We can go over it now!" Kate yanked her arm away. She'd been so sure Manny was still in the city. But every contact she'd made had come up empty. Something was wrong. She'd felt it for days. "Tell me, Martin."

"Just remember, it's not your fault." Her brother led her to the kitchen table. "Lissa, could you start some coffee?"

"Sure." The other woman slipped away.

Martin squeezed Kate's fingers. "Sounds like

this family has been on the run for a long time. What happens to them may be beyond anyone's control. You can't fix everyone's problems, Katie, no matter how hard you try."

The same way she hadn't been able to fix Martin's or her parents'...

Yet there her brother was, holding her hand. The way she should have stayed and held his ten years ago, regardless of how hard he'd fought her. And tonight he'd let Lissa into his apartment, even though he was clearly terrified of his feelings for her.

"What happened?" she asked again, loving him for everything he was starting to deal with. "I need the facts. I have to *do* something for these people. Please."

Martin winced. Lissa pulled up a chair beside them, leaving the lasagna and garlic bread and coffee to fend for themselves.

"We need to find them, Katie," he said. "It's not just about the kid anymore."

"I THINK IT HELPED Katie to have you here as a buffer," Martin said to Lissa, as he rubbed at the lightning bolt strobing behind his left eye. His sister had excused herself to the back of the apartment, close to crying and needing to hide. "Thank you."

Hell, it helped *him* to have Lissa there. He'd give anything to drag her into his arms and hold her until the pain and confusion went away.

"How close is your sister to this family she's trying to find?" Lissa asked.

"She's only met them a few times."

"But she seems to feel so responsible for—"

"Katie feels responsible for everyone. She's everyone's champion. She got you here tonight, didn't she?"

"Actually, I kind of hijacked tonight's festivities." Lissa left him sitting at the table, and crossed the room to pull the lasagna and bread from the oven. "Right after I insisted on stowing away at her place until I talked some sense into you."

"And here I've spent the evening worrying about *Katie's* overdeveloped sense of responsibility for people she can't save."

Martin had to fight like hell not to stare at Lissa's backside every time she bent to do something with the oven. His body's newly rediscovered appreciation for her soft curves was becoming more uncomfortable by the second. He shifted against the growing pressure below his waist.

"I don't want your help, Lissa."

h out and believe he could hold on to some-
g real.

"So, now you know it all." He made himself
y put instead of going to her and pulling her
o his arms. Soothing them both. "It's time for
u to head back home to your girls and stop
asting your time chasing something that isn't
oing to happen with me."

"Tony and Angie said they can watch the girls for
week or so," she replied, talking about her sister
and Stephen's ex-chief, who'd been married for
years.

"Lissa, look—"

"What makes you think my trip up here is all
about you?" she demanded.

"What? So, you've been dying for a vacation
to Atlanta, and this is your excuse to get away
from it all?"

"Something like that."

"Don't push this, Lissa." He was standing in
front of her and didn't remember crossing the
room. He reached for her before he could stop
himself, cupping her elbow in his hand, rubbing
her satin-smooth skin with his thumb.

"Why? Because you're already hard at work
pushing yourself?" She gazed around at the
memories of home, and her, that he'd dragged all

She walked slowly back to the table and set the
bubbling lasagna on a heat-safe pad.

"Maybe I can change your mind," she challenged. The spicy aroma of the Italian food wasn't
nearly as tantalizing as the serene smile she
flashed. "Like you and Kate and this Stephen
fellow are plotting to change this man Digarro's
mind about getting his son taken care of."

"That's different. My sister's patient is in more
medical danger the longer he's not being treated,
and he and his father—"

"Need to understand their limited options?"
Lissa's smile deepened at his scowl. "Yes, I heard."

"I've already chosen the option that works best
for me," he insisted, forcing himself to listen to
his own words while he was at it.

If he'd thought their problems were only
about the impotence, he'd have had her flat on
her back on the academy's couch despite
Stephen Creighton's surprise visit.

"Giving up on you and me isn't an *option*,"
Lissa countered. "It's quitting. Look how well
that worked for Kate."

"Katie didn't quit," he bit out. He'd let himself
believe she had for too long. He couldn't have
been more wrong. "She came to Atlanta to avoid
being a daily reminder to me that our father beat

on our mother for the entire twenty-five years of their marriage. And that Katie had known, and that she hid it to protect me. All those years she knew and never said a word. What does that do to a child?"

"Martin. I—"

"And I guess I knew it, too, in a way. But I pretended everything was sweet Southern pie, right up until I got my hands on my mother's journal and read it all in black and white."

I can't leave without the kids, and I can't support them on my own...

If I can just stop making Jim so angry...

At least if he's hitting me, the kids will be safe....

His mother had resigned herself to a lifetime of abuse for Martin's sake. For Katie's. Jim Rhodes had been an abusive bastard who'd let everyone around him lie to protect his secret.

Martin's entire childhood had been a lie.

"Martin, don't—"

"Don't what!" Now that Lissa was here, now that he was facing what he couldn't bear for her to know, *now* she didn't want to hear it? "After living the way we did, lying the way we did, it's no wonder Katie needed to move to the other side of the state. That her own marriage didn't work.

Do you finally get it? I'm no[...] of keeping a healthy relationsh[...] sister is. My only experience[...] watching my mother be silentl[...] day of my life!"

Lissa should have been sho[...] Running for the door. Instead, sh[...] hands on the table and pushed slow[...]

She walked into the family room,[...] fingers over his mother's favorite Sti[...] then the miniature rose bush on the ta[...] it. Lissa had brought it his first we[...] hospital. He'd been coaxing the thing to [...] winter, knowing the flowers would remin[...] her.

"So, your world wasn't as happy-go-lu[...] you made it out to be," she said. "So, there[...] mess—a lot of it. Don't you think maybe[...] figured some of that out over the last year?[...] know, right about the time you were hurt too ba[...] to keep pretending to be everyone's good-tin[...] guy?"

Martin nodded. Lissa always had been smarter than people gave her credit for. Smarter and more special than any of the "easy come, easy go" women he'd been with before. Special enough to tempt Oakwood's most determined bachelor to the way to Atlanta. "Except for how you're trying even harder to sabotage your recovery, it doesn't look like anything much has changed to me."

"So, I'm a coward." He was still hiding. He'd always be hiding from the things that had scared him as a child, and the things that still terrified him as an adult. "What do you think I've been trying to tell you!"

He should pull away. Why wasn't he pulling away?

Why wasn't she?

"You're not a coward." Lissa patted his arm, as if she were talking to a damn child. "You're human, and vulnerable, and you hate that. Too bad for you, it only makes me want you more."

"You're confusing pity with want. You—"

Martin's cell rang, from where he'd left it on the kitchen table beside the lasagna.

He let its electronic chant play on as he fell into Lissa's open expression—her need to believe in him.

When he couldn't stand it another moment, he limped back to the phone and flipped it open without looking at the display.

"Rhodes," he barked.

"Good evening to you, too, buddy," Tony

Rivers drawled in his slow, easy way. "Bad timing?"

"It'll do." Martin forced a calming breath. "You got something new?"

"Only that the DEA showed up today, asking the sheriff why our department was snooping into the Vargas cartel. If we'd heard anything about a Manuel Cubrero they're tracking."

"Did they say why the cartel might be tracking him?"

"That they weren't so eager to chat about. Sanders was cool. He passed the search off as part of our ongoing drug containment initiative, investigating recent arrests and gang activity. He waited until the Feds were gone before hitting me up for answers. But the DEA will eventually make the connection between me and you, and then you and that nurse who was involved with the Digarro case up there."

Martin winced as his headache spiked from annoying to excruciating.

"Yeah. Thanks for letting me know. And thank Sanders for me, too." He turned toward the den. "I'm sure Lissa wants to talk with her girls."

"Lissa's there?" Playing dumb was about the only thing Martin's best friend didn't do well.

"She already outed you and Angie as coconspirators." That morning, when Tony had relayed the DEA intelligence he'd dug up about Manny Digarro, the bastard hadn't breathed a word about watching Lissa's girls. "Save the covert moves for the Feds and go fetch her kids."

Lissa was already at Martin's side. She practically ripped the phone out of his hand. As far as he knew, she'd never spent a night away from Callie and Meagan. She should be home, not shadowing his ass. She should be where her girls needed her. Back at the job that had supported her family ever since her divorce from the county's biggest loser.

"No, hon," she said into the phone. "Mommy's interview is on Monday. I'll know more after that. But if the position at the bank is as great as it sounds, and the interview goes well, we will all be moving here as soon as I find someplace for us to live."

Lissa smiled up at Martin's shocked stare.

CHAPTER TEN

KATE WAS VISIBLY UPSET as she parked beside Stephen's car at the curb outside her condo. And she wasn't alone, as she approached his car. A familiar blonde walked beside her, not looking so *It's a Wonderful Life* herself.

Not that it mattered.

Stephen wasn't going anywhere until he was sure Kate was okay.

He got out to join them. Kate motioned toward the woman. "Lissa, this is Stephen Creighton. He's Manny Digarro's attorney."

"Mr. Creighton." Lissa slipped by and disappeared inside the building.

He got a brief glimpse of blue, watery eyes and a nose red from crying.

"She and Martin were together back in Oakwood," Kate explained, watching Lissa's departure instead of looking at Stephen. "She went over there with me tonight. Kind of fell apart on the way home. They still need to deal with a lot of things, and Martin's not ready."

Stephen waited, aware that he might be one of the things Kate didn't need to deal with right now.

"I can't believe you're here," she said, still standing too far away. "All the time we were at my brother's, during the drive back, I couldn't stop worrying about Dillon and his father, or wanting to talk things through with you."

"I'm a lawyer." He buried his hands in his coat pockets. "I'm the guy you talk to, when you need to talk things through."

"You're a good lawyer." She smiled, and he lost his next breath. "You're the Digarros' best shot, even though things are completely out of control. But… That's not the only reason I've been thinking about you all day, or all day yesterday." She ducked her head before looking into his eyes again. "I've been trying to decide if seeing you again is a good idea or not."

"And…?" He suddenly needed her to want whatever this was between them as much as he did.

"My brother's terrified of what he could have with Lissa." Kate laid a hand on Stephen's chest, her touch so light he couldn't stop himself from pressing her fingers closer with his own. "Neither one of us knows how to want people this way. We're not good at needing...."

"What do you need, Kate?"

Her touch slipped away. "I've been awful to you. Called you a liar and a user from the start. Because that's what I had to believe you were."

"Sounds about right." He chuckled. "Defense attorneys have a rep for fighting for the bad guys."

"Except you only take on clients you believe are innocent. And you're still fighting for the Digarros, long after another lawyer would have bowed out. I shouldn't have been blind to your commitment to Dillon and his father."

"But you were." And he'd let her be, long after he'd have set anyone else straight or stopped caring. "Mind telling me why?"

She hesitated. "As long as it was about Manny and Dillon, I had an excuse for pushing you away." Her fingers curled into his shirt. She stretched onto her toes, her mouth just an inch from his. "Instead of pulling you closer the way I've wanted to for days."

Stephen lost himself in her kiss, his fingers threading through her hair. He'd walked away from her yesterday, and ever since he'd felt the strangest sensation.

He'd felt alone.

But not now.

His hands smoothed down her spine. Her arms wound around his neck, then she snuggled closer, so trustingly she could have had anything she wanted.

Her bottom wiggled into his touch. Only then did he realize he was angling her hips against his. He shifted her higher, needing her…and he never let himself need anything but what he could make happen on his own. Just him.

But there was no *just him* with Kate in his arms.

He picked her up, turned and seated her on the hood of his car. Her legs hugged his hips, under his coat, applying sweet pressure while she deepened their kiss. This was the same woman who'd shied away just a few days ago. Now she was driving him crazy, as if she wanted to crawl inside his body.

He anchored his hands to the base of her head and tipped it back.

"Lissa," Kate said on a gasp. "She's—"

"Inside," he muttered, trailing kisses across her jaw to her ear. "Clothes. Too many clothes."

He tugged at her jacket's zipper. Thumbed the top buttons of her sweater free and slid icy fingers beneath the wool and the silk shirt beneath, smiling at her gasp. Then he gasped himself, at the softness of her skin—softer than the silk. He ran his fingers across the lacy edge of her bra, then under, until he was palming her nipple.

"Stephen…" She arched into him, her eyes wide, their green a glittering fire.

She pushed him away but held onto his coat as she stood and found her balance. Then she took his hand and tugged, giggling as they stumbled toward the condo.

He stopped at the sound and pulled her back for another kiss. She giggled again. Grinning like a kid, she yanked him forward.

Inside, her houseguest thankfully nowhere in sight, the January cold no longer whipping around them, he made fast work of her zipper and slid the jacket off her shoulders. The sweater followed. Then he was pressing her against the entryway wall, trapping her arms to her side. The touch of her lips and tongue rocked him, as if he were feeling it all again for the very first time.

This wasn't just sex. This wasn't just about taking the edge off. He didn't want to let Kate go when they were through, the way he'd walked away from every other woman in his life.

For the first time, he wanted more.

More of her…more of them…

"More," he growled as her hands ran down his chest, gripped his waist, then skimmed lower.

Careful, controlled, hands-off Kate.

"More?" She cupped him, not quite hiding the flicker of vulnerability in her expression. "How much more?"

"You have a houseguest, or you'd already have your answer."

"Lissa has her own room," Kate countered. "Looks to me like she's using it."

His body tightened at her open invitation. But he had to be sure.

"You have a lot going on already with the Digarros and your brother's situation," he said, hesitating.

"And the hospital *and* my volunteering at the shelter." She stiffened. "Look, if you're having second thoughts—"

His hand covered her breast. He gazed down at the nipple pebbling through her bra and the softness of her shirt. His body tightened at her passionate response.

"I want you to be sure, Kate. I want this to be right for you."

Right for both of them.

She smiled again. The mischievous sparkle in her eyes was the most beautiful thing he'd ever seen. Her soft laugh reached out to him, along with the arms she wrapped around his neck once more.

"Then let's find out how sure we are, together."

KATE HAD BEEN TOO exhausted that morning, too distracted, to tidy her bedroom. Then she'd had Lissa and the lasagna to deal with, and worry over Martin's reaction to their ambush. But as Stephen backed her into her room, and they tripped over the scrubs and shoes she'd climbed out of the night before, she couldn't have cared less about the uncharacteristic clutter.

The only light was from the bedside lamp she'd left on. Stephen looked even more amazing in shadow than he did everywhere else. She kissed the dimple in his chin and closed her eyes. But the golden-tinged shadows were still there, in her mind. Swirling through her entire body at his touch. Warming her where she hadn't even realized she was cold.

He wanted more.

And he made her want it, too, no matter how confusing and unsure things would feel in the morning. No matter what they still faced in their race to find Manny and Dillon before anyone else did.

She wanted this moment. She needed to believe she could handle the closeness he was offering.

They stumbled to the bed. When the back of her legs met the mattress, she pulled Stephen down with her, tightening her grip as his body covered hers.

"Gotcha," she whispered.

He shook his head. Slipped his fingers beneath the hem of her shirt and peeled it up, trapping her arms over her head, holding both wrists with one hand.

"Wanna run that one by me again?" The wicked glint in his eyes made her heart skip. Then his attention dropped to the lace and silk covering her breasts, and her heart forgot to beat at all. "*I've* got *you*, Kate Rhodes, and it's entirely possible that I might not let you out of this bed again."

"What gave you the idea there was anywhere else I wanted to be?"

She curled her legs around his, the same way she had outside. Only this time she had gravity on her side. He fit perfectly against the part of her that was throbbing for attention. His hold on her hands released. He popped the clasp on her bra, slid it free and lowered his mouth to taste.

"Magic." Stephen pushed away just far enough to drag his dress shirt over his head without unbuttoning it. "You taste like magic."

Kate helped him with the cuffs that had caught at his wrists, until she could toss the warm cotton away. She ran her hands down his chest, around his sides and then back up the muscles rippling across his back. She nibbled her way to his neck.

"You taste like you have too many clothes on," she challenged. "Last one naked makes breakfast?"

He shuddered, and not just because she'd whispered the last sentence in his ear. It hadn't escaped her that he wasn't the type of guy who typically stuck around long enough for the coffee to brew the next morning.

"Breakfast for two, huh?" He let his gaze roam downward, as if contemplating the pros and cons of her offer.

"Uh-uh." She slid from beneath him until she was kneeling in the middle of the bed—topless, but still wearing her jeans and socks. "Breakfast for *three.* I have a houseguest who likes her eggs over easy. I'm scrambled, with a handful of shredded cheese thrown in."

He rolled to his feet.

"Cheese is going to cost you extra." His hands hooked in the waist of his pants, just above his belt buckle.

"Um…" Sidetracked by the amazing way he was filling out said pants, she had to shake her head to get her mind back on target. The man was a walking distraction! "Extra? Does that mean you're conceding defeat?"

"Nope. Just raising the stakes. I'm greedy."

Promises, promises.

"Breakfast and dinner, then?" she countered.

"Both homemade?"

"Or dinner at a five-star restaurant of the winner's choosing."

"Homemade, it is." He winked. "I'll bring the wine."

"On your mark."

His stance remained comfortably relaxed.

"Get set."

She tensed at his mocking grin.

"Go!"

She ripped the button loose on her jeans, and had them and her panties down in a flash. Stephen's jaw dropped. He grabbed her by the knees and yanked her back to the mattress, pulling the last of his clothes off, their competition completely forgotten.

"I win," she purred as he caressed her from her calves to her thighs.

He shook his head. Kissed the inside of her knee. She felt his slow, Southern smile all the way to her soul.

"We both win," he said. "Tonight, we both win."

"Is THE JUICE fresh-squeezed?" Kate asked as she floated into the kitchen the next morning.

She'd gotten very little sleep for the second night in a row, but she'd never felt better.

"The juice is from the carton you keep in the door of the fridge." Stephen had pulled on his dress slacks but had left his oxford shirt unbuttoned.

He was using a wire whisk to give a mixing bowl of eggs what-for.

"Let me guess." She sat and sipped her juice. "Busy, rich lawyers make their own breakfasts these days just to prove that they don't take their status too seriously."

He shrugged. "No sense having to get dressed and go out for anything more complicated than coffee. So, I took a few classes and learned the basics."

Whatever he wanted, Stephen simply set his

mind to and got. And last night, he'd set his mind on her. She smiled at the memory.

"*Basic* smells good." She inhaled the delicious scent of her victory. Closed her eyes to savor it.

How long had it been since she'd felt this loose? This comfortable with a new day, let alone with a near-stranger making himself at home in her kitchen. Except Stephen hadn't been a stranger since they'd first met at the hospital. Something deep inside them had connected. Something she hadn't ever expected to find.

She didn't want to leave the kitchen—or the moment, which a part of her wasn't sure she'd be able to hold on to once they walked back into the real world.

"Eat." He laid a plate in front of her. "We've got a long day ahead of us."

He'd piled the plate high with eggs and bacon cooked to perfection. And there was plenty remaining for Lissa, who hadn't made an appearance yet. Kate lifted a fluffy, buttery forkful and saluted her indentured servant before taking a bite.

"You're as good as your word." She'd scooped up another mouthful before she'd swallowed the first. "We'll have to wager more often, at least until my waistline outgrows my wardrobe."

"I'll buy you a new wardrobe." His naughty leer down the neck of her bathrobe, under which he'd insisted she wear nothing, made swallowing her next bite difficult. "Losing to you is a pleasure."

She covered her snort by sipping her juice. He sat and dove into his own eggs.

"You loathe losing." She crunched on a strip of bacon.

"Actually, I don't lose." He set his fork down and rested his forearms on either side of his plate.

"And that makes this morning…".

"About having you right where I wanted you, without having to ask if I could stay."

"So, you let me win last night, so you didn't have to admit to wanting to stick around?" She laid her fork aside. "That's a shade manipulative, don't you think?"

"I'm a lawyer." Stephen's expression turned distant for the first time since she'd walked up to his car last night. "Exactly what did you think I do for a living?"

She blinked.

"You help people who are being chewed up and spit out by the legal system," she countered carefully.

"I help myself." He sat back and folded his

arms, demonstrating just how sexy a man in rumpled business attire could look. "Doing what I do for other people—"

"Is all about you?" She clenched the table-cloth.

The real world could have at least waited until after breakfast to make an appearance.

"I'm not some romantic hero," Stephen warned.

During the night he'd been more generous, more patient, more involved than any man she'd ever been with. Before that, he'd waited for her to work through her confusion over the Digarro case and her brother. He'd given her time to trust him. To trust herself.

What exactly *was* a hero in his book?

"Do you always tell women that you're a using son of a bitch over breakfast the morning after?"

"I'm never around for the morning after."

"Maybe I've manipulated you, then."

"Maybe you should listen to what I'm saying before you go another round with me tonight."

"Tonight?"

"I want tonight." He took her hand, held fast when she would have shied away, unsure of his mood. "I want tomorrow morning. Damn it, I want you, Kate, any way I can get you, and I never play to lose. But I don't want you to wake up tomorrow or next week or next month—"

"Next month? Let me get this straight. You're a bastard, but I'm going to let you stick around for a month?"

His low opinion of himself, hidden deep beneath the successful veneer of one of the top legal minds in town, translated at some level to a low opinion of her.

Didn't he get that?

"No. I'm—" he let her go and ran his fingers through his sleep-rumpled hair "—I didn't—"

"Think I was smart enough to figure out for myself whether I should trust you or not?"

"You're smarter than I am, Kate, but—"

"But with men, I'm too inexperienced?"

"Not that I could tell last night, no." There was that leering glance again, the one that made her want to shove reality back out of the kitchen door. "But—"

"Then what exactly is *my* problem. What makes you think you have to warn me off, so I don't make the mistake of falling under your spell? I get it. You're a real person with your own agenda. I mean, you even have selfish motives for the work you do, just like everybody else. What was I thinking!"

Stephen studied his cold plate of perfectly prepared food.

"I don't do relationships well," he explained. "My work keeps people at a distance, but I still get to do them some good. Which is a step up from my parents, who spent their trust funds on themselves and didn't give a shit about anyone else. But, doing the caring, loving thing isn't my strong suit. Never will be."

And there it was—the connection she hadn't been able to put her finger on. The unspoken understanding she'd felt in Stephen even before she'd let herself trust anything he said or did.

"Well, since my father beat the hell out of my mother, when he wasn't belittling her so he could keep her thinking she was worthless without him," Kate said, her voice rough, "and since my mother hid the signs of their dysfunctional home life from everyone in town but me, and since I hid the whole thing myself, I guess I have my own reasons for keeping people away."

Stephen sat straighter in his chair.

"Kate—"

"I don't have the first clue how to trust my feelings for anyone, either," she continued. She wasn't stopping until it was done. "Not even my brother, or the only man who pushed through my crap long enough to get me to marry him. So, I guess that makes me a closed-off, manipulative user, right along with you. Maybe you're the one who should be careful. Breakfast the morning after, with a serial one-night stand like me?" She *tsk-tsked* as she stood and walked to the sink to scrape her food down the drain. "Not a wise move, counselor."

Stephen stepped behind her. He wrapped an arm around her waist, braced the other on the edge of the sink and curled her into his warmth.

"I thought we already established that you're smarter than I am," he whispered against the spot on her neck, just below her ear, that he'd discovered was ticklish. "And I'd bet money you can count on one hand the number of one-night stands you've had. Not that I wouldn't take another night with you any way I could get it."

He turned her until their bodies aligned. She was close enough to kiss the beard stubble lining his jaw.

"So." She rubbed her palm across his chest—she'd discovered a few sensitive spots of her own. "You're as bad a judge of playmates as I am, then?"

"I'm not playing." His hand covered hers. "And neither are you. But…"

"You're scared."

Strong, independent, successful men who could bend anything in their worlds to their will didn't get scared. But Stephen was.

"Of hurting you, yes." He pulled her fingers to his lips, kissed them, then let her hand drop to her side.

She lifted it right back to his mouth and began tracing his lips. Her breath caught as he sucked the tip of one finger between his lips.

"Or maybe," she offered, "you're trying to scare me away, so you get to control how much this hurts *you* when it's over?"

Stephen took a step back.

"Have some personal experience with that tactic?" he asked.

"My ex held out longer than I thought he would," she admitted. "But the day Robert filed for divorce, I took my first easy breath in years."

"Because you like getting hurt?"

"Because it was better than waiting around for him to prove me right."

"About what?"

"That I'm not enough. That the people I'm trying to love will always get hurt, no matter what I do, because I'm just not enough."

The shocked glimmer in Stephen's expression

softened to understanding. He pulled her head to his shoulder. "You couldn't be expected to solve your parents' problems. And it sounds like you did everything you could to protect your brother, no matter how much keeping quiet hurt you."

"But it wasn't enough."

And Martin was still paying the price. They both were.

She melted into Stephen's strength. Distracting herself, she trailed her lips across the strong column of his throat.

He lifted her chin.

"When your brother ran, he came here." Stephen turned and steered her out of the kitchen, back toward the bedroom. "He moved into an apartment less than ten minutes from you. And the first time he needed help, you were the one he speed-dialed."

"He was hurt."

"He needed you." Stephen stopped in the middle of her bedroom and drew her to her toes, so they were face-to-face. "You were there for him. He knew you would be."

"Yeah, he needed Nurse Kate."

"No, he needed *you*." Stephen kissed the tip of her nose. "Your heart. Your grit in a fight, and, yes, your ability to face the world honestly. He may not have been ready for that before, but he needs it now, and you're there for him. *I* need it, though I can assure you I need a whole lot more."

"*More* can be a very scary word," she said, as she tried to believe.

"Yes, it can be."

"As scary as the possibility we won't find Dillon and his father before they run for good…?"

"We'll find them. And we'll work through the rest of the scary stuff, too."

Stephen's bone-deep confidence gave her hope enough to ask…

"And this—" she motioned to him, then back to her "—whatever this is. What about us?"

"*Us* is what I want to work through the most. As long as you're sure."

He waited, his expression guarded.

The choice was hers.

"Yeah." She nodded. "I think I'd like that. A lot."

He nodded, too. Took a deep breath, and looked over her shoulder to the master bath.

"We've got a lot of ground to cover today, if we're going to take Atlanta apart looking for our runaway Colombians. How big is that shower of yours?"

"Want first dibs?"

"Actually, I was thinking we could save time if we showered together. I'm always willing to sacrifice personal comfort for a good cause. How about you?"

She linked her arm around his and led the way.

"I just love the way your logical mind works."

"THANKS, MAN," Stephen said over his cell to Neal as he pulled fresh jeans and a pullover sweatshirt from his chest of drawers. "I'm sorry to keep busting into your time off."

The man had been gone less than forty-eight hours. "It's a Small World" was playing in the background, for heaven's sake!

"Don't worry about it," Neal assured him. "The girls have their day planned, and I've got my laptop and wireless cell card back at the hotel. Do what you have to do to find Manny and his son. I'll head back and work with Kelly on the INS precedents."

Stephen and Kate had stopped at his apartment on their way to the Midtown Shelter so he could find something to wear besides trashed business clothes that looked like they'd been slept in. While she was hanging out in his living room, he'd bitten the bullet and called in reinforcements.

Use all your available resources, Neal kept saying. *I don't expect you to be a one-man show.* And he'd been as good as his word. If anyone could find them what they needed to protect the Digarros, it was Neal.

"What about the rest?" his boss asked.

"Martin Rhodes has his ex-chief on board, pushing DEA to play enough of their hand to agree to a meeting—that is, once I have Manny back and know what the hell we'll be meeting about. Jenkins is working whatever he has to internally to convince the APD it's in their best interest to protect the Digarros while they're in town. If a Colombian drug lord's visiting with a hate-on and an eye on doing some damage, we're looking at a violent scene. Local police should be willing to extend themselves a little to keep that from happening. Especially if it's a good bet a federal agency will be footing the bill soon."

God forbid the point of protecting the family actually be to keep a sick kid's father alive, not to mention getting Dillon the medical care he needed. But Stephen would work whatever angle he had to. Whatever got the job done.

Except where Kate was concerned.

With her, he wanted it all. No quick deals. No angles. He'd laid it all on the line that morning, showing her everything he had to offer, and everything he didn't. And she hadn't flinched.

She was as off balance as he was, but she'd come out swinging.

"So, what's your next step?" Neal asked.

"What?" Stephen yanked himself back into the conversation.

"Are there any new leads?" Neal prodded.

"Not yet. But we'll dig something up. He's got to be with someone either connected with the homeless community, or to his life in Bogotá, or both. Kate and I are going door-to-door today. If we find someone who even looks like they've got something to hide, we know the buttons to push."

"Manny Digarro is pretty damn lucky Kate thought he was hurting his kid. Otherwise, we'd never have known to look beyond his immigration problems."

"Yeah." Stephen sat on the end of his bed.

As lucky to have met Kate as he was.

"Let me know when you find the guy," Neal said. "I'll keep in touch through Kelly."

"You got it."

Stephen hung up and began stripping off the clothes he and Kate had made a mess of—the kind of mess he realized he'd welcome every day for the rest of his life.

He'd told her he wasn't sure if he could make

a relationship work long-term. That he couldn't make her any promises.

What a cop-out!

He'd finally found something he could be more passionate about, more committed to, than the legal system he'd built his life around. He finally knew what loving someone that much felt like. And the thought of losing that love was even more inconceivable than losing Manny and Dillon Digarro to whatever demons were hounding them.

"You ready to go?" Kate called from the living room, eager to get started—to keep fighting the latest battle she refused to give up on, despite the odds against them.

He rushed into his clothes, grabbed his tennis shoes and headed for the den.

"Let's do it," he said.

CHAPTER ELEVEN

DILLON HAD NEVER STOLEN anything in his life.

He felt the wallet in his pocket bumping against his leg. The manager at the shelter had left it on his desk that morning—beside the phone. Dillon had snuck up from the basement to call Kate. He'd taken the wallet instead.

He'd pay the man back. He'd left his car in exchange. It wasn't worth much, but it was all he had to trade. He'd heard Papa telling the manager they should have left days ago. The manager wanted to loan Papa money for the bus. But Dillon was still too sick for the bus. Papa wouldn't leave.

So Dillon was leaving instead. Nurse Kate would help him get better. Maybe over the phone she'd have said no. But if he just showed up, what choice would she have?

Waving down a cab wasn't easy when you were short, with one arm in a cast, ribs that ached and zero energy. But Dillon kept waving his good arm and trying not to put weight on his sore ankle. He had to get out of there. Someone would notice him missing any minute.

He ripped a shrill whistle, just like Papa taught him. The next yellow car that passed by screeched to a halt at the end of the street.

"Take me to the Midtown Shelter," he said after scrambling into the backseat.

"Huh?" the guy behind the wheel grumbled. "You got any money, kid? 'Cause I ain't taking you nowhere, if you can't—"

Dillon tossed the wallet through the scratched-up plastic window separating him from the front seat.

"What the—" The man opened it and stared, then slowly nodded. "Okay. Where did you say you wanted to go?

There was all kinds of ID inside, but that didn't seem to matter. If Dillon had learned anything watching Papa and his boss in Colombia, it was that money took care of things.

"The Midtown Shelter." He laid his head on the seat.

What if Kate wasn't there…?

He'd worry about that later. He'd head for the

hospital next. Whatever. As long as he found her.
As long as he got better.

As long he and Papa could get out of Atlanta
before it was too late.

"If you hurry," he said, "someone will pay
you more when we get there." At least he hoped
they would.

The driver pulled a bill from the wallet and
tossed it back. Dillon let it land on the seat beside
him. He didn't even bother to check to see how
much the man had taken. It didn't matter, because
they were finally moving.

The tires screeched, as the driver left rubber
behind.

KATE HADN'T MISSED a shift at the hospital in
years—not since she'd rushed to Oakwood after
Martin's shooting. But she'd begged Marsha to
cover her hours for the rest of the weekend, so she
and Stephen could track Manny and Dillon
together.

They weren't going to stop until they found
them.

She glanced across the Midtown Shelter's
kitchen. Stephen had busied himself with the industrial coffeemaker, brewing steaming coffee
for every volunteer in the place, while Kate talked

with anyone she could find who might have seen the Digarros.

They were a *they* now. The fact was both amazing and terrifying at the same time.

"So, first we'll hit the other shelters in town." He leaned back against the counter and crossed his legs. "We'll have to work on description. Who knows what name they'll be using."

"I wish we had a picture to show people. Though Dillon's cast and bruises should be enough to identify him. I just—"

Stephen stepped closer and drew her head to his shoulder, same as he had after their shower, when she'd had too long to sit and think about their slim chances of actually finding the family, no matter what they did differently today.

"We'll come up with something." His fingers caressed the sensitive skin on the side of her neck. His gentleness, the unexpected playfulness that cropped up when she least expected it, it was all too new. Too perfect. "We'll leave notes on the message boards that only Manny would understand. Somehow, we'll talk him in, so you can take care of Dillon."

"And you can figure out a way to get the Feds working with Manny, instead of against him."

She closed her eyes against Stephen's kiss.

"I'll figure something out," he promised. "I'm a damn good lawyer. So is Neal. Trust me."

She wrapped her arms around his waist, distance never less important to her. "I do tr—"

"Kate?" Randall poked his head through the kitchen door. He tried not to look interested in the sight of Kate in Stephen's arms. "There's someone out here asking for you."

Regulars looked for her all the time. Any other morning, she'd be happy to offer whatever TLC she could. But—

"We're heading out in a few minutes." She moved out of Stephen's reach. "Would you mind taking care of it for me?"

"You'll want to see this one," Randall insisted. "I think it's the kid you've been looking for."

"Dillon?" Kate raced out the door, Stephen at her heels. "Dillon!"

He was slumped in a chair, away from the others who were waiting for breakfast to be served. He wasn't just pale. His complexion was on the pasty side of grey.

"Kate!" His familiar accent was the sweetest thing she'd ever heard. "I knew you'd be here."

"Hi, kiddo." She lifted him from the chair, appalled at how easily she could do it. "Let's find you some place you can rest up a bit."

An average ten-year-old should weigh at least seventy-five pounds. The hospital scales had put Dillon hovering around sixty, and he'd clearly dropped even lower over the past few days.

"Excuse me." A burly stranger she hadn't noticed followed as she walked toward the office. "The kid said something about more money if I got him here fast."

"He drove me," Dillon explained while Kate settled him on the office's cot. The center kept it made with clean sheets in case someone needed to rest in private.

Stephen scowled at the cabby's outstretched palm, pulled out his money clip and peeled off a bill without looking to see whose picture was on it. It was an overly generous tip, if the man's double take was any indication.

"I'll need a receipt for that," Stephen said.

Kate shot him a questioning look as the cabbie ripped a blank receipt off a pad, handed it over and beat a path to the door.

"So I have his contact information if we need it," Stephen explained, pocketing the slip of paper.

"Where did you get the money to take a cab?" Kate brushed Dillon's sweaty bangs back, kneeling beside him.

Guilt washed over his features, mixed with the

kind of worry no ten-year-old should have to shoulder.

"Here." He held up a man's wallet.

Kate took it and flipped it open to find the ID of another shelter's manager. Nodding, though she didn't understand what was going on, she passed the wallet to Stephen.

"We'll make sure it gets back to its owner," she assured her young visitor.

"I didn't want to take it, but—" Dillon glanced at Stephen and the still-hovering Randall.

"Could you give us a minute?" she asked Randall, shaking her head when Stephen motioned with his shoulder, asking if he should back off, too.

"Sure," Randall said and left.

Dillon swallowed, his eyes round as saucers as he sized up the man now kneeling beside the cot along with Kate.

"You remember Stephen from the hospital, right? He brought you that car from your dad."

Dillon jerked his gaze back to her. "You were really mad at him. You were mad at Papa, too."

"I didn't understand how much he and your father wanted to help you. I was wrong." Her glance of apology to Stephen was rewarded with a soothing caress at the back of her neck.

"Stephen's been helping me look for you," she explained. "He's trying to make it possible for you and your dad to stop moving around as much as you have. To stop hiding."

Dillon blinked. She could see him weighing her assurances against survival instincts that should also be foreign to a kid his age.

"We have to hide," he said, his accent stronger as his fear visibly rose. "Papa and me… He… He could be in a lot of trouble if we don't. And he won't leave Atlanta while I'm sick. Kate, you have to help me get better. We have to leave."

"Your father's in trouble with the authorities here in the United States?" Stephen asked.

Dillon didn't look away from Kate as he nodded.

"And he's also in trouble with someone who's following you from back home, isn't he?" Stephen's patience finally earned him Dillon's attention.

The boy nodded again.

"But Papa won't run this time." Dillon fingered the hem of the blanket Kate had tucked around him, then he kicked it away and sat up with a wince. "It's because of me! It's always because of me. He's going to get caught because he doesn't think I can keep going."

"You can't," Kate said gently. She urged him to lie back down. "You're hurt pretty badly, and you're going to need a lot more time and rest before you can do much of anything. You shouldn't even be out of the hospital."

"I got myself here, didn't I?" Dillon challenged.

Kate smiled at his tough-kid comeback.

"You couldn't even get back out of that chair a minute ago, Dillon. You need to stay put for a while."

"My…" He sniffed, then wiped at his nose with his good arm. "My dad can't get caught because of me. He…he…"

"How much danger is he in, son?" Stephen cupped Dillon's shoulder. "Is it the man he worked for back in Bogotá? Is that who's after you?"

Dillon nodded. "He's going to find us if we don't go."

Admitting his secret seemed to steal the last of Dillon's strength. He melted into the mattress.

His eyelids drooped, blinked, then opened more slowly, only to close again.

"I knew I could trust you, Kate," he said as he drifted off.

Stephen's hand slipped away from the thin shoulder as he stood.

"Still beating yourself up for ruining his life?" He drew Kate to her feet beside him. "The kid needed help, and he ran to you."

She glanced down at Dillon. She needn't have worried about him overhearing. He was out cold.

Stephen motioned for her to follow him to the hallway. Once there, he shut the office door behind them.

"He should be in the hospital," she said.

"How many people do you think saw him come in here?" Stephen was staring at the floor, the way he often did when he was thinking hard. "Besides the cabby—and all that man saw was the green Dillon and I flashed under his nose."

"This place is crazy in the morning." A bomb could go off in the shelter's dining room, and no one would think anything awry, as long as the chow line opened on time. "It's a stroke of luck that Randall even recognized Dillon."

"So if we were to get the boy out of here quietly enough, how likely is it that anyone but Randall would remember seeing you here with Dillon?" When she didn't immediately respond, Stephen smoothed her bangs from her eyes, his expression serious. "How much do you trust this firefighter friend of yours?"

"I've worked with him for years. I'd trust Randall in anything." She realized where Stephen's questions were leading. "People are going to know Dillon's resurfaced as soon as he's readmitted to pediatrics."

"He's trusting you to help him without putting his father at more risk."

"Helping him means getting him to a doctor."

"Not at Atlanta Memorial. Dillon's a minor. Technically, his only parent let him wander away. I'm assuming the hospital would be required to file a report. That means APD would start looking for the boy's father all over again, and that'll put Manny in even more danger from—"

"The people Dillon said are after them." Dear God. "And if there really is someone closing in on them, and they get their hands on Dillon before they find Manny…"

"And they're as dangerous as I think they are? They won't blink at using him to get to his father and whatever Manny knows or has that they want back so badly."

Kate glanced through the door's window, at the brave little angel sleeping inside. What kind of courage did it take for a child to confront his demons head-on, the way Dillon had? A whole lot more courage than Kate had had when she'd been hiding from her family nightmare for years. Or all morning, when she'd been having a running conversation with herself over not being freaked by how fast things were moving with Stephen.

"We can't keep him here, or at either of our houses." Stephen drew her around to look at him again. "Too many people know we're searching for the family. It would be too easy for someone to figure out. But I already have an APD contact looking into a safe house. And you know a doctor who could look after Dillon, until I can get things squared away."

He waited, letting her decide. Clearly wanting her with him, but giving her the chance to walk away from the risk they'd be taking.

And suddenly, the rightness of trusting Stephen's instincts made it seem like a no-brainer. They were going to do what they had to do, together, and they were going to make this work.

"I'll page Robert at the hospital," she said. "I'm sure we can stay the night at his house. Marsha can bring me whatever we'll need to monitor Dillon's condition. I'll keep him quiet and make sure he rests. But he needs more tests. He's—"

"Very sick. I know." Stephen's relief tempered

his worry. "We'll get through this as fast as we can. First, I've got to get to Manny before he does something stupid. He must be going out of his mind worrying about Dillon. Once I have his whole story, I'll take it to the INS or the DEA or whoever will promise protection the fastest."

"And then?"

This could still blow up in their faces.

"Then you and I, and my boss and my APD contact and Martin's DEA contact and whoever else we need to get involved will do what I love best about my job." Stephen's gaze held hers. "We're going to manufacture this family a miracle."

CHAPTER TWELVE

MARTIN GRITTED HIS TEETH and pushed against the Nautilus weight platform, extending his legs.

"Balance the weight between both legs," Carmen Lender said.

Not that you could call fifty pounds *weight*.

"When do we take off the training wheels?" Martin asked around a grunt. "Back home I used to press two-fifty on a machine just like this."

"If the weight's too much, we'll take it down." Carmen eyed the sweat coating Martin's body. "More reps is the key, not the resistance."

"The key—" Martin pressed again, ignoring the shaking in his right leg "—is for me to be able to take a shower without having to call my big sister to get my ass out of the tub."

"You're still not going to let me schedule any X rays, are you?" Carmen had been pissed when she'd discovered the tenderness in Martin's hip and he had admitted to not getting checked out after his fall. "You could have broken something."

"I'm just…" Martin clenched the handgrips on either side of the seat. His legs slipped the last few inches, sending the weight crashing down. "Sore."

Carmen calmly removed the pin from the stack of weights. There'd be no more reps that afternoon, not even *with* training wheels.

"You're going to permanently injure yourself," she warned, "if you don't stop expecting the impossible. You've made amazing progress, but—"

"I need to accept my limitations. Yeah, got it."

Martin swiveled off the bench, grabbed his crutch and stood, remembering all of Lissa's warnings to the same effect, her voice full of love and fear and belief that he could get through this. That they could still have a chance.

A chance he was tempted to believe in again, more each time he saw her.

"Let's work on the bars," Carmen advised. "Then we'll cool down with some stretching and a massage."

She always started him with stretches, before he walked with the aid of a torture device that resembled a gymnast's parallel bars. Then came the weights, and finally, at his insistence, back to walking. Because no matter what he could do on a mat or a piece of weightlifting equipment, it didn't mean dick if he couldn't walk without the crutch that felt like it had become a permanent part of his body.

He positioned himself between the bars. Carmen stood to the side, spotting him.

"Just a few steps this time," she cautioned. "You've pushed a bit too far already."

Ignoring her, he set off, tentatively sliding—*sliding*—his right foot forward, while loosening his hold on the bars and lifting his hands. Letting the right leg bear his weight, he inhaled and raised the left off the ground. His right leg promptly gave out, its muscles spasming as the ground rushed up to meet him. He caught the bars with his arms, and Carmen supported him as much as she could, while he struggled to get his legs back under him.

Every curse word he'd ever known came tumbling out, one right after the other.

"Martin!" Suddenly, Lissa was holding him on the side opposite Carmen. "Are you all right?"

"What the hell are you doing here!" His body leaned into hers, as if he had no say in the matter. And to make things worse, the area immediately south of his waist responded to her nearness again.

"Can't you get it through your head, I don't want you here."

Clearly his body did, but that didn't mean he intended to do anything about it, even if Carmen had given him the all-clear to enjoy his reawakened libido. Hell, he couldn't even put one foot in front of the other.

"Back on the bars," Carmen said now. "I'll get your crutch."

His damn arms were weak as noodles as he fought to support his weight on his own.

"Get away from me," he growled at both women. "I'm fine."

Carmen must have been satisfied. She turned and retrieved his crutch, then headed for the side room, where she'd massage the kinks out of his muscles on a low table he'd barely be able to roll off of once she was through.

"Five minutes, and your ass is mine again," she said as she went. "Your hip's already tight. You're not going anywhere tonight until I've worked you over from head to toe."

And he wasn't going anywhere near her table until his raging hard-on was under control.

"You can't be here," he said to Lissa in as close to a civil tone as he could manage.

"Martin…" She felt so right beside him, touching him.

It was bewitching. Terrifying. It made him want to throw his crutch away and lean on her instead. Forever.

Except, even with his manhood intact, he was still half the man she deserved.

"I…" He sighed. Time to cut to the chase. "I can't handle you being here, making me feel the things you do, when…"

"You don't like the way I make you feel?" She glanced down, then let her gaze slide back up his sweat-slicked body. "Wanna run that one by me again?"

"Yes, I'm hard." He clenched his jaw. "It seems all you have to do is walk in the room the last couple of days, and I want you."

She smirked.

"Be careful, Martin, or you might just turn my head."

"Fine, as long as I'm turning it away." He eased out from between the bars and, on his one-and-a-half good legs, went to finish the day's physical therapy.

Lissa, of course, put her two bewitching legs to work and cut him off at the pass. Leggings… She was wearing black leggings beneath her coat and the oversized sweater that hugged her thighs and butt.

"Damn it, get out of my way!"

"I've done that long enough." Fury heated her expression. "I don't care how afraid you are of me or us or whatever it is you're feeling, I'm not going anywhere tonight, or any other night, until I damn well want to. And right now, I want to be *in* your way, more than I've wanted anything else in my life."

It wasn't a good idea—he might not be able to get up again—but he headed for the nearest bench and seated himself on it with a groan.

He couldn't bear being close to what he couldn't have, no matter how many times she offered him his dream come true.

It was Lissa's turn to sigh.

"Is it really possible?" She was standing in front of him.

"Is what possible?"

"That you're more afraid of me than you are of never having complete use of your body again?"

Martin leaned his head back against the wall and closed his eyes. He still saw her, though. She'd always be in his mind, even after she'd given up and was gone.

"Anything's possible," he conceded.

At Lissa's soft touch on his cheek, he opened his eyes. She trailed her fingers down his chest and the ancient muscle shirt he'd worn. Then those legs he had nightly fantasies about were straddling him as she slowly, carefully lowered herself to his lap. His instant response jerked beneath her.

"The question is, why?" she purred.

"Why?" He gripped her waist, filling his hands with her sleek softness. His fingers tightened against his body's demand to sample more. "Because I don't have the strength to move you off me and walk away, not even for your own damn good. And screw sex. I can't be what you need outside the bedroom, either, and we both know it."

She rocked forward, her expression turning dreamy as she draped her arms around his neck.

"I know this feels wonderful." She lowered her head enough to lick the inner curve of his ear. "And I know your big, bad heart—and how much you're worried about hurting me—turns me on even more than your body does."

Her lips fluttered against his throat. His hands began to roam.

He'd touched her, held her, made out with her

back in Oakwood. But that had been a long time ago, when he'd been carefully courting her and hiding the parts of himself she shouldn't have to deal with. There was nothing careful about the need coursing through him now.

He wanted to be the man for her, the one she couldn't leave behind. The way she'd always be the woman for him. No more lies. No more secrets.

"Get away from me." He ordered his hands to stop their descent, dropped his arms to his side and opened his eyes.

"Why?" She didn't budge, her eyes wide. "So you can console yourself instead of dealing with the dirty work of living with what you really want? You refuse to let yourself reach for happiness, Martin. That would mean trusting that together you and I can handle the good stuff, as well as whatever's bound to go wrong next."

A not-so-hushed cough was their only warning.

"Would you two mind postponing the *good stuff?*" Carmen asked. "I've got dinner plans, and—"

"No problem." Lissa rocked forward and back again, then she slipped to her feet.

But she didn't back off. She just stood there,

only an inch away. Martin's hands reached for her before he realized what he was doing. He clenched them. Pressed them against the bench. As he stood, his chest accidentally brushed hers.

Like hell it had been an accident.

Her next breath took his away, his body was so sensitized to the feel of her against him. And she noticed.

She'd always noticed everything about him. About them.

"We're finishing this tonight," she promised.

"EXPLAIN TO ME AGAIN how keeping a sick child away from the hospital is a good solution?" Robert asked Kate in his living room. "His father doesn't know where he is, and you don't have legal authority to make Dillon's medical decisions. You're taking an awfully big risk."

Kate had known Robert would help, even though it meant another endless discussion of how she let taking care of everyone else consume her life. Stephen was off somewhere scraping together a miracle. She could endure her ex-husband's good-intentioned nagging.

"You're a brilliant doctor," she countered. "Dillon couldn't be in better hands."

"I'm a surgeon."

"I'm assuming that means you had to go to the same medical school as pediatricians."

"The boy needs a specialist, and—"

"And you have a huge Buckhead home, where no one's going to come looking for the Digarros anytime soon," she said in a hushed voice.

Dillon was in one of the upstairs guestrooms, and voices had always carried in this monstrous place.

"This should be *your* huge home, Kate." Robert planted his hands on his hips. He'd just rolled off twelve hours in surgery, but he hadn't hesitated when she'd asked him for help. He'd examined Dillon before Kate tucked him into bed, and he'd agreed to let them stay for as long as they needed. "I offered it to you in the settlement."

"How would I pay for a place like this?" Her wave encompassed the two-story room.

"With the money I instructed my lawyer to give you, along with the house."

"Nah." Kate eased into the overstuffed, leather couch, and picked up one of the grilled cheese sandwiches she'd made for herself and Dillon as a late lunch. "The money and the house are better off with you."

She'd agreed to taking her car, enough money to cover a sizable down payment for her condo, and the retirement savings and investments she'd made during the marriage. Anything beyond that would have felt mercenary.

It would have felt like letting Robert take care of her still, which was what she'd needed to escape from in the first place. Now here she was, running to him, and of course he'd taken her in.

"It's not your fault, you know." He sat beside her and took the other half of her sandwich.

He bit, barely chewed and swallowed. Then he looked down, as if just noticing what he was eating, and took another bite. When they'd been together, if Kate didn't cook, he'd go for days living on whatever came out of the surgical floor's vending machine when he shoved quarters in.

She waited for him to swallow, then handed over the remainder of her half and headed for the kitchen to make more.

"I know the Digarros' situation isn't my fault," she said. "Can we please not dissect this?"

Robert leaned against the counter while she turned on the burner to reheat the pan.

"I mean our divorce." He sighed at her glare. "I knew I wasn't giving you what you needed in the marriage, but I let us go on pretending. It was easier than forcing the issue, and—"

"We were both busy?" Keeping *busy* had kept them together for years.

"Truth was, I didn't want to talk about it any more than you did," he admitted. "In the long run, you were more honest than me. That's why you asked for the ending we both knew was right."

Kate buttered bread, laid the expensive, premium cheese Robert preferred on top and turned the sandwiches into the pan.

The wall clock ticked away.

"I'm a lousy partner, Robert. And I'm lousy at being saved from myself. You on the other hand—" she flipped the sandwiches so the other sides could brown "—can't stop yourself from wanting to help me."

"I wasn't trying to save you." He crossed the tiny space separating them. "I was trying to love you."

"Turned out to be the same thing at the time." She hadn't been ready to be over the past then, which had made happiness with Robert impossible.

"And now?"

Robert and Stephen had been polite when Stephen had dropped Kate and Dillon off. But her ex had been throwing protective vibes around like a force field. The closer Stephen stood to her, the deeper Robert's concerned frown became.

"Now… I'm not sure…."

"Well, that's an improvement, I guess." Robert visibly relaxed at the idea of another man maybe being what he never could have been to her. "You two actually make sense together, in a way. Creighton looks as shell-shocked as you do."

Kate slid a sandwich onto a plate. She handed it to Robert, then scooped up her own and took a warm, gooey bite.

"No one's where they thought they would be this afternoon." She and her ex were having a friendly chat about her new guy; Dillon was falling asleep beneath six-hundred-thread-count pima cotton; Martin was most likely finishing up his therapy under Lissa's watchful eye, and Stephen… Stephen was out doing what he did best, but he wasn't doing it alone this time. He was trusting not just her but a whole team of people to help him pull off the biggest deal he'd ever tried to negotiate.

"But do you like where you are enough to want to be there tomorrow?" Robert prompted.

For him, being a surgeon was everything. He lived for it. He regretted their divorce, but it's not as if he missed being married all that much.

His life was exactly where he'd always needed it to be.

Kate had thought hers was, too.

That morning, Stephen had said he wanted even more. More passion. More working together. More supporting one another and understanding things they shouldn't be able to but did, no matter how little time they'd spent together.

But did she?

Falling in love, loving a man who admitted to trusting the emotion even less than she did would be taking the biggest risk of her life.

"I KNOW THE DIGARROS stayed here," Stephen said to the manager of the Second Ponce Homeless Shelter. *Clifford Reynolds,* according to the name plate on his beaten-up desk and the ID in the wallet Stephen still held. "Dillon told me this is where they've spent every day and night since leaving the hospital. I'm Manny's attorney. His son is safe and with friends of mine, and I thought perhaps his father would be relieved to know that. Maybe want to speak with the boy."

"And I hope you find him, so you can relay your message." Clifford's "I'm not following you" act, ever since he'd invited Stephen to sit across from his desk, would have been convincing—except for one minor detail.

Stephen reached over a stack of paperwork and picked up a familiar plastic race car.

"Manny gave this to me when his son was hospitalized. He trusted me enough to take it to Dillon when he couldn't, and Dillon trusted me and his nurse enough to track us down, because he knows his father is in danger."

"Does this look like a dangerous place to you?" Reynolds asked.

"Don't mess things up for this family by playing dumb. None of us have that kind of time. I've got to see Manny. He and his son need to stop running and start dealing with whatever happened before they left Colombia."

The other man sighed, his fingers steepled in front of him. His attention shifted to the back of the cluttered room that looked to be more of a storage bin than a manager's office. Stephen turned as a door he hadn't noticed squeaked open. Manny Digarro stepped out, a gun in his hand.

"You're going to take me wherever that nurse has my son." Manny closed the outer office door. "Then the two of you are going to stop looking for us, stop asking questions about us, and Dillon and I will leave Atlanta for good."

Stephen stood, his hands raised.

"Put that away, Manny," Clifford said in Spanish that he evidently thought Stephen wouldn't understand. He stood, too. "You promised if I let you stay, there'd be no danger to anyone here. I protected you. Do the right thing and keep your word."

"Right?" Manny answered in the same language. "The only *right* thing is protecting my son. He's all I have. My last chance to do what's *right*. I don't care about anything else anymore."

"Not even getting yourself killed?" Stephen asked in flawless Spanish. Manny's eyes narrowed. The gun shook in his hand. "How is you being dead, or deported back to Colombia to get dead, going to help Dillon? How is threatening me going to protect you from Vargas? I know the INS is the least of your worries. Dillon knows it, too. He came looking for Kate so he could give you the chance to get away."

Manny stepped closer. "Tell me where my son is."

"He's in a private home, under the care of a doctor."

"What doctor! Is he okay?"

"He's weak, but he seems to be fine. I don't know how long we can keep him there. I have a local police contact willing to go to his boss and ask for protection, a safe house, until we can figure something out with the federal authorities. But he can't do that until I know what's going on. You're going to have to trust me, Manny."

Stephen held up the wallet Dillon had stolen, carefully showing it to his gun-wielding client, then tossed it to Clifford.

"Tell me how much is missing, and I'll replace it," he said in English.

"If you already know the kind of danger we're in—" Digarro's English was as good as Stephen's Spanish "—then you know the protection of your police doesn't interest me. It's too late for that. My chance to go to the authorities was gone long before we ran from Bogotá. Tell me where my son is."

"Running isn't the answer," Stephen insisted. "How long do you think you can keep it up with a child as sick as Dillon? If you're being hunted by your old boss, the authorities here may be your only shot at staying alive."

"I have to agree with the man." Reynolds stepped around the desk and held out his hand. "Give me that gun, my friend. I bet it's not even loaded. My cousin in Colombia says you're a good man. Stop this. Listen to what your lawyer has to say before it's too late."

"It's already too late for me!" Manny lowered the handgun, opened the cylinder to show that there were in fact no bullets inside and tossed it to Clifford. "I've tried to protect my son. It's always been about protecting Dillon and getting him what he needs. Clearly, I can't do that anymore. You're right, Mr. Creighton. It's good my Dillon is with an American doctor who will know what to do for him. It's better this way."

Stephen studied his client's body language. Manny's resignation, when just a moment ago the man had been furious.

"You knew," he said. "How long have you known Dillon has a life-threatening medical condition?"

Manny's eyes filled with tears and the kind of hopelessness that made a man look old. He slid into the chair Stephen had vacated and dropped his head into his hands.

"For several years." He rubbed his eyes with the heels of his hands. "Why do you think I've done any of this?"

"Running to the States?" Reynolds asked.

"Agreeing to work for that bastard Vargas for as long as I did. Hiding his money. Earning him millions in interest, so he could keep killing other people's children with drugs."

Manny swallowed, his expression one of self-loathing.

"But if Dillon was getting help in Bogotá, why run?" Stephen asked. He needed answers. The man's regrets would have to wait. "And why is Vargas after—"

"Vargas killed one of his generals in front of me!" Manny glanced to the shelter's manager, then shook his head as he looked back before Stephen could hide his shock. "No matter how good I am with money, I was a liability after that. I knew too much. I'm a witness to cold-blooded murder, and I know every investment the man's made in the last five years."

"Vargas won't stop until he's found you, will he?" Stephen's concern for Manny and Dillon's safety shifted to fear, for both of them and Kate, when she heard the truth.

"I'm as good as dead if his men find me." Manny's voice caught. "I know Dillon needs treatment, but I thought I could find someplace safe…. I thought I could take care of him until…"

"And now Dillon's trying to take care of you," Clifford reasoned. "He's run to these people, so you can stay together once he's better."

"He won't get better," Digarro countered.

"Of course he will, my friend," Reynolds insisted.

"Promise me you'll make sure the doctors take care of him," Manny begged Stephen. "I'll make sure the danger chasing me never comes near my son again."

"I'm working on the protection." Stephen picked the toy car up from the desk and handed it over. "For both of you. Dillon's not going to be okay if he doesn't have you, Manny. That's one bright boy you've raised. He found his way to Kate with almost no information to go on. If you run without him, he'll try to find you, too. Once he's in the open, there will be no one to protect him."

Manny stared down at the car—it had been his promise not to leave his son. To always come for him, no matter what. "How could I have let myself forget that when you make a deal with the devil, sooner or later, you always lose."

"Well, this time, you're making a deal with me," Stephen countered, reaching out his hand. "And the only price is trusting that the best shot you and your son have is to stick together."

Digarro hesitated, then shook his hand.

"Why are you doing this?" he asked. "Why are

you putting yourself and your nurse friend in danger to help us?"

It was a fair question.

Thanks in large part to Kate, Stephen was beginning to understand the answer himself.

"Kate and I want to make sure you can be the father you need to be for your son," he explained. The type of father every little boy should have. One who'd sacrifice anything, risk everything, for his child. The kind of parent Stephen hoped to be one day, with the most amazing woman he'd ever met. "We're not stopping, Manny, until we've made that happen. Tell me what happened in Bogotá, all of it, so we can find a way to make this right for your family."

CHAPTER THIRTEEN

MARTIN DUCKED HIS HEAD under the shower spray, feeling like a fool for hiding in the rehab center's locker room. But the alternative was facing Lissa again. He had no doubt she was still waiting out front, and he had absolutely no idea what to say to her.

He didn't want things between them finished. But he couldn't—wouldn't—dump all his shit on her, either.

He raised his head and let the hot water rain down on him.

Now is what's important, Katie had said. *What we choose to do with now.*

When he'd read his mother's diaries, every childhood memory he possessed had shifted from sunny and light to a darkness he hadn't known how to deal with. He'd moved away, just like his sister, but he'd surrounded himself with reminders of the make-believe picture he still wanted his past to be. And where had that gotten him?

The memories had taken over, until he didn't know how to live without them.

A secret, hidden part of him hated his parents for what the abuse and the lies had taken from him. He'd even let himself blame his sister for a while.

A gasp drew his attention toward the door leading from the locker room to the communal shower.

Lissa's gaze jerked up from its journey down his body. His back was mostly turned, but enough of his profile was visible for a bloom of embarrassment to rush to her cheeks.

"I… You…" she stuttered. "Carmen left. She said you were alone back here, and there's only the receptionist out front waiting to close in another hour. Everyone else has gone home for the night. So I… I…"

His anger from earlier resurfaced.

She what?

What did she think she'd find when she wandered back into the otherwise deserted locker room?

He turned toward her, completing the show. He did nothing to hide the hard evidence of both his temper or the desire that raged higher every time he saw her.

"Well?" It was time to end this once and for all. His hand slid to the safety bar set in the tile. "If you've got something more to say, say it. Then get in your car and go home to your family."

To her adorable girls, their friends and the content life he felt light-years away from.

She turned. His instinctive urge to follow left him biting back a curse, as he clung to the bar that kept him balanced without his crutch.

Let her go, man.

Except Lissa stopped at the door that led back to the locker room, shut it and turned the lock, then she set her purse and jacket on one of the benches just outside the shower area. With her back still to him, she removed her soft, fuzzy sweater and laid it over the bench, then her hands went to the bottom of the clingy shirt she wore beneath, and—

"Lissa, don't—" The protest lodged in his throat as she pulled the shirt off, leaving her in nothing from the waist up but a fire-engine-red bra.

Sleek muscles and soft skin bunched and glided in feminine perfection as she kicked off her shoes and slid out of her leggings. Her panties matched her bra—the combination of the two, along with her petite, delicate figure, was the cul-mination of the midnight fantasies that had kept Martin awake and frustrated all last night. Except now, his waking dream was real.

"Lissa…" His hunger turned her name into a growl.

She turned, her uncertainty clear. But so was the strength of will that far outpaced his. She unhooked her bra and let it fall, then skimmed out of her panties, stepped out of them and kept walking, stopping only when she was standing directly in front of him. And there she waited, exposing every vulnerable inch of her body to his gaze.

Heat sizzled through him. The shower's steam kissed their skin, shifting in lazy patterns, wrap-ping them in a moment disconnected from every-thing and everyone else. He should grab his crutch and walk away. Leave her once and for all, even though his rejection, after she'd risked so much, would be humiliating for her.

But his mind, his soul, refused to budge.

He wanted one more taste of the dream.

"You need to get the hell out of here," he warned.

"You owe me a shower." She took one final step closer. Made a point of looking her fill before laying a palm on his slick chest. "You promised me one a year and a half ago, remember? The day you were shot. I've been waiting patiently until you were better. Are you going to try and convince me that you're not...up for it?"

"Do you really think whether or not I can get hard is our biggest problem?" He inhaled as her hand slid upward.

Her fingers brushed his cheek.

His hand nearly slipped off the support bar.

"No." The word, her voice, was as smooth as her challenging smile. "Our biggest problem is that you can't let yourself be honest with me."

"Damn it." He grabbed her arm, his grip rough. "Why can't you get that I'm trying to protect you?"

He dragged her under the shower spray, pushing her hair back as the water danced off them both. She leaned into his touch, closed her eyes and gasped when he angled her face up and lowered his. But instead of kissing her, he shook her until her eyes opened.

"You want me to use you, Lissa?" he cajoled. "That's what this would be, because I'm not going back with you. I can't go back. The man I was in Oakwood doesn't exist anymore."

She rubbed her cheek against his, her eyes closed again, her lips searching for his mouth.

Damn, she was so sweet, so trusting, it was killing him.

His fingers clenched in her hair.

"Don't, baby," he begged. "Don't do this. Don't want me, when—"

"Stop telling me what to feel!" She wrapped her hands around the back of his skull and dragged his mouth down to hers. She kissed him hard. "Stop telling me what to want."

"Baby—"

"Stop babying me!" She pushed away and stood naked and shivering before him. "Stop trying to warn me off, like I'm looking for an excuse to run screaming."

She placed her hands on her hips, the pose an erotic temptation all by itself.

"I want you," she continued. "All of you. I'll still want you twenty years from now, even if you send me away and we never get to see how good this could be. If you want to worry about something, worry about how *you're* going to feel then, knowing you threw all this away."

He swallowed. Pulled her closer after having pushed her away for so long. Tears shimmered in her eyes, stabbing at him, as she let him fold her against his body.

He leaned his forehead against hers. "I'm trying to protect you…."

"From whatever's inside you that you think I

can't handle?" She sounded hurt, scared. But determined to understand.

"I have to deal with this crap." It terrified him, the thought of casting shadows on her life, instead of the joy she deserved. "I don't want you feeling trapped—"

She wound her arms around his neck and arched her hips against his.

"Who's trapping who?" She kissed him softly this time. "I'm right where I'd want to be even if we'd just met for the first time. You know how I know? You still care about me and my girls. You still care about your sister and what's important to her. You're a good man with a huge heart, and I love you. And that's never going to change."

He blinked. Stared at the relaxed acceptance in her expression. Blinked again.

His grip on the support rail was like a vise, while his other palm gently roamed to her bottom to cup her closer. He felt her quiver in response.

"Does this mean I'm finally getting my shower?" Her next wiggle was a naughty thing. So was the wicked quirk her lips curved into as he squeezed her bottom.

"I can't think of anything I want more." His heart pounded as the truth broke free. "But..."

"No buts." Lissa dipped under the shower spray and took his bar of soap. She smoothed it over his chest. "I'm not going anywhere," she promised. "Tell me you can believe that, Martin, and I'll take care of believing the rest, for as long as it takes."

As long as it takes...

He took the soap from her trembling fingers and the spark of courage from her gaze. Smiling his first real smile in what seemed like forever, he trailed a path of lather over one trembling breast, then shared the caress with its twin.

"Damn straight you're not going anywhere," he growled.

He set the soap aside, sat on the tiled seat, then pulled her onto his lap. Her legs settled around his waist, until their bodies were perfectly aligned.

He finally saw fear in her eyes. A flicker of insecurity that made her so much more precious to him, because she relaxed against him anyway, trusting him.

Lissa had given him everything—her heart, her strength, even her pride. Whatever it took to get them to this moment.

For the rest of his life, she'd never doubt his feelings or her value to him again.

"THANKS, MARTIN. I'll let him know." As Kate hung up Robert's kitchen phone, a feminine voice on her brother's end of the line asked who'd called.

She smiled, despite the fact that Stephen had called half an hour ago to say he was on his way with Manny Digarro, but he hadn't shown up yet. It was hard not to smile when her brother called her *Katie*. When he didn't seem to mind that she'd phoned to check if everything was all right.

Things sounded more than all right. Safely back at his apartment after therapy, Martin wasn't alone tonight.

He'd heard from Tony Rivers, too. As good as his word, Tony had put a bug in the DEA's ear about making a deal with Manny for whatever the man had on his old boss—hopefully it was something important enough to trade for his and Dillon's protection. A lot rested on that. But if something as damaged as Martin and Lissa Carter's relationship could work itself out, anything was possible.

The doorbell rang. She heard Robert head from the den to answer it. Before she could get there herself, the sound of Stephen's warm voice urged her to close the distance faster.

"I've got some work to do in the office," Robert was saying as she skidded into the entryway to find a disheveled Manny Digarro at Stephen's side. "Mr. Digarro, you're welcome to use any of the guest rooms you like. Kate knows where everything is."

He left them to fend for themselves, thinking nothing of opening his home to a total stranger for the second time that day.

"Mr. Digarro." Kate took Stephen's outstretched hand, clinging to him in both relief and concern. His frown was at odds with the fact that Manny was back with Dillon, where he belonged. "I can't tell you how sorry I am about all of this. I've caused you and Dillon so much trouble."

"Please, don't, Ms. Rhodes." Manny shook his head. "You've taken care of my son. You've kept him safe. You'll make sure he gets well. That's all that's important."

His uncomplicated forgiveness filled Kate with a sense of rightness she hadn't felt since that morning, when she'd been wrapped in Stephen's arms.

Stephen squeezed her hand.

"May I see Dillon?" Manny's request was formal, despite his desperate search of his surroundings.

"Of course." Kate made herself move away from Stephen. "He's upstairs sleeping. If you'd like to rest with him for a while…"

"Yes, thank you."

She motioned Manny up the stairs, then followed. Stephen's cell phone rang, and she glanced back, her steps slowing. He ducked into the den before she could read his expression. But his body language had been enough.

He might have spent the afternoon doing the impossible—tracking down Manny Digarro and persuading the man to trust them—but the miracle they needed for the Digarros was far from complete.

CHAPTER FOURTEEN

TWENTY MINUTES LATER, father and son reunited and resting as comfortably as possible, Kate retraced her steps to find Stephen still on the phone, pacing the length of the den.

"Keep digging, Kelly." He clicked his cell closed. "Neal's been working over e-mail with my assistant, scouring INS precedents where the defendant was permitted to stay in the country for medical reasons."

Stephen shrugged off his coat, took Kate's hand and urged her to join him on the couch.

"What's wrong?" she asked.

He absently rubbed her palm, as if he was trying to decide where to start. "The best we have so far is that the INS might delay Manny's deportation until Dillon's condition is stabilized. The boy's medical situation should be enough to keep him here indefinitely, but we'll have to approach the INS as soon as possible so they can begin to process a provisionary visa. The jig will be up anyway, as soon as he's readmitted to the hospital."

"But if you contact the INS, they'll—"

"Want to know where Dillon's father is." Stephen was shaking his head. "If only we knew how long it'll take to get the DEA on board…."

"Martin said Tony Rivers is pushing his DEA contact to do more."

"We need local operatives involved now." Stephen stood and began to pace. "Manny's holding on by a thread. It took forever for me to convince him to come here—that there's no chance anyone would connect Robert to him or his son, at least not before we get them to the safe house Curt is working on with the APD."

"Where else would Manny be?" Kate brushed at the chill racing down her arms. "He's talking about running? Alone? He wouldn't do that to Dillon."

"He would to protect him." There was a hint of acceptance in Stephen's voice.

Resignation.

"How is losing his father going to protect Dillon? He thinks Manny hangs the moon. I'm supposed to be making him *all better,* so he and his father can keep running together. If Manny leaves without him… I don't even want to think what that would do to Dillon's recovery. His condition's already so weak."

Stephen came back to the couch and sat, concern etched in every line of his frown.

"Manny told me what happened in Bogotá. He probably has something the DEA could use. But—"

"So he'll tell the federal authorities whatever they want to know, in exchange for being able to stay in the U.S."

"He's too scared to wait."

"Scared of going back home? You said you could hold the INS off for a while, until—"

"No. Scared of the Colombians that are tracking him. Scared of them 'taking care of things' before the DEA can make a decision."

"Taking care of…" Kate swallowed. "The Colombians who are after Manny don't want to bring him back to Bogotá, do they?"

"No." Stephen's touch gentled even further. She could feel how much he wished he was wrong about whatever he was about to say. "They want to make sure he—or what he knows—is no longer a threat to a very dangerous, well-financed man. And if I don't get Manny some police protection soon, if the DEA doesn't want his information badly enough—"

"Then Manny's going to make sure he's nowhere near his son when the Colombians find him."

It was exactly what she should have known Manny would do.

It's always been about me, Dillon had said.

"Curt's telling me there's word on the street that Vargas's men may already be in town," Stephen explained. "Clifford Reynolds at Second Ponce heard from some of the other shelters that you weren't the only one asking about the Digarros. Manny and Dillon are in a lot of danger."

"Because of me." Kate pushed off the couch, following the facts to their next logical conclusion. "Let's forget for a minute that we're talking about Dillon losing his father. What's going to happen when the INS or the DEA want to know where Manny is, and he's nowhere to be found. You're on record as his lawyer."

Stephen stood, too, and sunk his hands into the pockets of his perfectly pressed jeans. He stared at the toes of his high-priced sneakers.

"You're going to catch hell," she answered for him. "I haven't just fixed things nicely for the Digarros, I've screwed you, too. Does Neal Cain know any of this yet?"

Stephen nodded his head. "I've filled him in, and he's behind whatever I decide. Even if he wasn't, I'd do what I have to do. I promised Manny I'd keep Dillon safe, no matter what it takes."

"To hell with the consequences of interfering with a federal investigation? You'll be prosecuted, all because I dragged you into this mess."

"*I* pressured *you* for us to work together," Stephen reminded her. "You didn't beg me onto this case. Dillon is a child. He deserves a life filled with security and love. You saw that, and you helped him the only way you knew how. Now, it's my turn. Don't you realize, your passion for helping a total stranger's child is part of why I love you? And I—"

"Don't say that!" The ugly feelings raging inside Kate congealed into something so desperate, she could hardly speak. "You don't love me."

"I don't?" Stephen scowled. "Why? Because you don't love me back, or because you're still scared of your own feelings?"

"You're the one who should be scared." She motioned to the house around them. "Robert loved me. He'd still do anything in the world for me. And I think I started running from him right about the same time we exchanged vows."

"What does that have to do with us?"

"I'm not any better at feelings and trusting what to do with them than you are. I've shut out my husband, my brother…everyone I've known my entire life. Except at work. I had the work thing nailed. I was helping people at the hospital and the shelter. Now I'm destroying lives left and right even there, and you want to love me!"

"What exactly do you think would have happened to Dillon if you hadn't intervened? And today, without your brother and his contacts, I never would have talked Manny in."

"In to what? Accepting that he can't stay with his son?"

"Oh, get over yourself, Kate!" Stephen turned to stare out the window. Shaking his head, he pivoted back. "Manny was over his head years before he walked into your homeless shelter. The Colombians were probably already on his tail by the time he hit town. But now he's trusting us, he's trusting *you,* which gives him and Dillon a chance."

"That man's nuts if he thinks he can trust me."

She felt it welling up, from the empty place inside she'd never been able to fill. The place that had lost faith in her parents and herself the day she'd walked in on her father brutalizing her mother—then a few hours later, had sat down with them to a nice, quiet family dinner.

She began to pace, coming closer and closer to Stephen, until she was standing directly in front of him.

"*You're* nuts if you think you can trust me with your heart," she insisted.

"Why?" He sounded mystified, as if he'd really believed they could make it.

The way she'd been trying to believe all day.

"Because *I* don't trust me!" She swallowed, fighting to keep from throwing up. "It's only a matter of time before I blow it with you, just like I've messed up everything else. Before I say or do whatever it's going to take for you to realize that this is impossible. It's better to end it now, before—"

"End it!" Stephen's expression was everything she'd dreaded from that moment back in the diner, when she'd begun falling for him.

His eyes drained of all warmth. Emptied, until he was once again the calm, collected attorney she'd first met at Atlanta Memorial.

"According to you," he said, pinning her with a pointed finger, "it never really started. What does that make last night and this morning about? Just a quick-fix release, to tide you over for another few years—until the itch gets out of control again? Any excuse is fine, is that it? As long as you can walk away clean when things get too real. Even if it means using the Digarros' shitty situation to do your dirty work."

"I'm not using the Digarros. I'm not using you! I'm trying to—"

"Sure you are. The same way you use your past every time someone gets close enough to make you nervous. That makes you a coward, Kate. Not the fighter I thought you were. I should know. I've been the same kind of coward since I wasn't much older than Dillon. Then I met you, and I was just stupid enough to believe…" He went to the couch for his coat, slipped it on, pulled something from his pocket and stared at it for several seconds before looking up. "I really thought I'd found someone who understood…who needed something, someone, to believe in again, as much as I did…."

He placed whatever he'd been holding on the coffee table and headed for the foyer.

"Stephen—"

She should let him go.

But she was rushing after him instead, needing to hear him say he believed in her again, despite everything. Needing him to keep saying it, until she could find a way to believe herself.

"I'll be back once I have confirmation from Curt on the safe house," he said over his shoulder, his tone professional, impersonal. "I'll get in touch with Martin and have Tony Rivers and his DEA guy contact me on my cell. Any problem taking another day off to keep an eye on Dillon if we need you to?"

"I'll take more personal time." She had an endless supply that Robert and Marsha had been hounding her to use. "Whatever you need me to do."

Stephen turned, the pain in his expression adding to the ache in her heart.

He deserved to be loved and taken care of. And he'd let himself need both from her.

"I never meant to hurt you," she whispered.

He nodded. All emotion drained from his features.

"I'll be helping Kelly at the office." He opened the door. "If there's a legal way to keep Manny and Dillon together, we'll find it."

The door closed behind him and the house grew silent.

She headed back to the den, and that's when she saw the car Stephen had left on the table.

The plastic, dime-store car Manny Digarro had bought for his son. It had been a father's promise to always come back.

She and Stephen would keep fighting to give Manny a chance to keep his promise. But they weren't fighting together anymore.

Kate had never felt more of a prisoner to her past. Without Stephen by her side, wanting to believe in what they could have as badly as she secretly did, she'd never felt more alone.

And *alone* didn't feel safe anymore.

"WE'LL BE THERE SOON," Stephen said to the scared family in the backseat of his car the next morning.

He turned down the side street that would deliver Manny and Dillon to the APD safe house.

As soon as the DEA had come on board, Jenkins had been able to formally request APD protection. An APD escort had met Stephen at Robert Livingston's place, and the officers had been on Stephen's tail ever since they'd left Buckhead behind, on the way into the city.

Kate had wanted to come. She'd wanted to speak with Stephen privately. But he'd said no to both requests.

DEA would be at the safe house. Stephen had fed the agent he spoke with sketchy high points of what Manny knew. The Digarros had a chance because Manny had hesitantly agreed to give this meeting a try. The INS had been temporarily called off. But Manny would be quite literally talking for his life once they arrived at their downtown destination. There were still no guarantees.

If things went wrong, Kate didn't need to be there, feeling even more responsible for the family's dilemma.

And even if things turned out as right as Stephen hoped they would, *he* didn't need her there, looking so worried—for *him* as well as the family they were trying to protect.

It was clear she cared, that she maybe even loved him, too. But she didn't trust she could be good for someone. Or maybe him loving her was the real problem.

Before he'd said those words, he'd been a risk, but not to her heart. Now, he was one more person she was sure she'd let down, because she thought following her heart would always end in hurt.

I love you.

He'd never said it to any woman. He couldn't remember far enough back to when he'd felt safe enough to think it, to say it, even as a child. But he'd been certain he was safe with Kate.

Another APD cruiser was waiting when he pulled to the curb beside the apartment building. Curt and his partner exited the car as Stephen and his passengers did, along with the officers who'd followed them over. Two men in suits emerged from a nondescript sedan two cars down. DEA, no doubt.

The gang was all there.

"Let's get everyone inside," Curt said as he looked up and down the quiet, upscale street. "No sense taking any chances."

Stephen turned to the Digarros. A movement behind their police escort, a car pulling away from the curb, caught his eye a split second before the sound of squealing tires made everyone else turn. The car raced by, the faces of its occupants a blur. The guns they held were the only thing Stephen managed to focus on.

"Get down!" Manny roared. He knocked both his son and Stephen to the ground as gunfire erupted from every side—from the hitmen, from Curt and the other officers and from the DEA guys.

Pain sliced through Stephen as he dropped and covered Dillon as best he could. Manny's grunt, his gasp for breath as he fell against Stephen, confirmed that he'd been hit, too. Metal struck metal in a deadly crash. The hitmen's car collided with others parked just a few feet down the curb.

Then silence reclaimed the street, punctured only by the sound of footsteps racing toward them. And Stephen could do nothing more than lie on the ground, his body curled around a sobbing child's, as blood seeped through his clothes.

CHAPTER FIFTEEN

KATE RACED INTO the E.R., not bothering with the reception desk. She slowed enough to pass through security and its scanners, then headed for the double doors that led from admissions to the trauma area. It took three tries to get her card to swipe, then she was running inside, desperate, her heart breaking.

There was a shooting at the safe house, Martin had said when he'd phoned. *The Digarros didn't make it inside. Either someone was tracking your lawyer friend, or something got leaked at DEA. Sounds like APD shut everything down pretty quickly, but there were some injuries....*

Her brother hadn't been able to tell her anything more, other than that more than one ambulance had been called, arrests had been made and that everyone who needed patching up was on their way to the hospital. Stephen's friend Curt had been the one to contact Martin, and both of them would meet her at the hospital as soon as they could. Robert had been listening to her end of the phone call, and he'd already grabbed his keys by the time she'd hung up. After breaking every speed limit on the way over from his house, he was outside navigating the packed parking deck, while she sprinted toward a reality she wasn't sure she could bear.

Were Dillon and his father all right?

She hadn't heard from Stephen. Was he okay? Was he—

"Kate!" Marsha called from the other end of the hall.

The trauma unit was in chaos, as usual. Less critical cases were "fast-tracked" to an entirely different area, leaving the specialist in trauma to triage and focus on at-risk patients.

"I came down as soon as I heard about the shooting." Marsha zigzagged through the maze of staff and patients, gurneys and other equipment, to get to Kate. "What happened—"

"Where is he?" Kate didn't wait for the answer. Ducking into each alcove, she stopped only long enough to check the identity of each patient being treated.

Marsha hustled behind her. "Dillon? He's upstairs. They're admitting him to pediatrics, and there's a slew of APD on the floor making everyone nervous. What happened?"

Kate pulled her friend aside as EMTs rushed in from the ambulance bay, pushing a gurney and calling out the patient's stats for the doctor hurrying alongside.

"Dillon's okay?" Kate asked through the weight of fear still pressing down on her. "Then he wasn't shot?"

"No." Marsha grabbed Kate to keep her from rushing off. "He's perfectly fine, just weak. But he's terrified and he won't talk to anyone. Kate, what happened? Were you with him—"

"No." Because Stephen hadn't wanted her there. "I have to find him…."

She wrenched away from her friend and checked the next examination area, knowing that the farther she went, the closer she was getting to the rooms reserved for only the most critical patients.

"Dillon's upstairs," Marsha insisted, still close behind.

"Not Dillon." Kate turned the corner, her heart and her feet stopping at the sight of the man being treated on a gurney in the crowded, overfilled hallway outside the largest trauma suite. "Stephen!"

He was looking away from her, into the trauma

room, while an intern set stitches in his shoulder. The sleeve of his shirt had been cut away to expose the wound. What was left of the expensive knit was covered in blood. Too much blood to have come from his injury alone.

Kate's gaze rose from cataloguing his condition. Relief at seeing her warred with something else in his eyes. Something that looked too much like giving up to belong to Stephen.

"Are you okay?" She rushed to his side. The intern who'd been working on him shifted away—either finished with his task, or uneasy with the tears Kate couldn't keep from falling as she wound her arms around Stephen. "Martin said there was shooting at the safe house."

When Stephen didn't hold her in return, she eased away.

"They were waiting for us when we got there." He strained to see through the window separating him from the trauma suite. "Are we done?" he snapped at the intern Kate hadn't realized was still hovering.

"Move around too much, and you'll open your sutures." The younger man ripped off his gloves. He looked more than ready to rid himself of his surly charge. "The bullet only grazed you, but you need an updated tetanus booster, and we're starting you on a round of antibiotics. Stick close. A nurse will find you when she's ready."

Stephen pushed off the table. He was weaving through the milling bodies in the hallway, then into the trauma room, before Kate could say another word.

"Stephen, what—" She halted just inside the door, recognizing the man the trauma team was furiously working on.

"We'd just gotten out of the car," Stephen said, watching as the doctors and nurses fought to save Manny Digarro's life. "APD was there. Local DEA, too. But before we could… Before we could even get inside…" He rubbed a hand over the blood that had dried to the front of his shirt. Kate realized it coated the back, too. "Manny saw them first. He pushed Dillon and me to the ground, but we didn't make it down before they started shooting."

They?

"The Colombians." Kate jumped at the sound of Manny's heart monitor flatlining.

"He's coding!" A doctor began CPR immediately. "Get the cart over here. Someone intubate him. Now!"

"You're going to have to wait outside." A nurse

pushed them both toward the door, so he could reach the crash cart behind them.

Robert was there when they stepped into the hall, standing next to Marsha.

"I hear you gave him CPR on the scene," he said to Stephen, which explained how Stephen had gotten blood all over the front of him. Manny Digarro's blood. "If he makes it, it'll be because you kept him alive long enough for the EMTs to get there."

"If he dies, it'll be because he trusted the wrong man to keep him safe." Stephen had eyes only for the trauma team's efforts.

He was so still, he didn't seem to be breathing, until the doctor shocked Manny's chest with the defibrillator. Stephen blinked at the jarring sound, drawing a breath that he didn't release until the monitor began to beep again.

Manny's heart caught an uneven rhythm.

"Stephen." She laid a hand on his shoulder, feeling the tension that still ruled him. "It's not your fault. You've done everything you could—"

His head snapped toward her. His hard glare dared her to finish her sentence. She was parroting back to him exactly what he'd been trying to tell her last night—when he'd said he loved her, and she'd thrown the words back at him. He'd trusted her with something he'd likely never said to another person, and she'd tossed it away.

He shrugged off her touch. It was clear he wasn't interested in hearing anything she had to say.

She'd promised herself last night that if she got another chance, she wouldn't make the same mistake twice. That as soon as she could, she'd talk to Stephen. Beg him to—

"Mr. Creighton." An enormous man appeared beside them. As if his severely cut dark suit and the hint of a firearm beneath his jacket weren't clue enough, he flashed a badge. "Agent Conrad, sir, DEA. If you have a few minutes, I need to take your statement. It's important that we know whatever Mr. Digarro may have said to you about the Vargas organization. It's the only way we can be sure to keep your client and his son safe."

Stephen's focus stayed locked with Kate's a moment longer. The word *safe* hung in the air between them. In that moment, she was certain she could see every fear and hope Stephen had wanted to face with her, reflected back in his too-blue gaze. Then the top-notch lawyer inside him took control, and he turned to Agent Conrad.

"I'm sure the two men who attacked my client

while he was supposed to be under your protection," Stephen began conversationally, "can tell you anything you want to know about the Vargas cartel."

"The two suspects who ambushed you today are dead, but we don't believe they're the only lieutenants Vargas sent to deal with Mr. Digarro. The more information we have on the situation, the better we'll be able to predict Vargas's next move. It's in your client's best interest—"

"I'll decide what's in my client's best interest." The timber of Stephen's voice hadn't changed, but his smile promised zero cooperation unless the federal agent made it worth Manny Digarro's while. "If he survives his injuries, he and his son will both need costly medical care and the kind of deep relocation that will cost even more."

"I'm not authorized to make any deals—"

"You sure as hell sounded authorized on the phone when you set up that meet-and-greet you handled so poorly. You're responsible for my client taking this field trip to heart failure!"

"And the man may not make it." Agent Conrad's jaw clenched, then he exhaled slowly. "We need your statement, sir. I'm afraid waiting is not an option."

Kate had never seen Stephen look more calm, more in control.

"Digarro told me everything he knows," he said. "Everything you need to go after Vargas. You want that information before Mr. Digarro is able to give it to you himself, then start dealing. I want to see a relocation plan. I want assurances from someone about three levels over your head, and I want them now. Dillon Digarro deserves to be safe, just as much as he deserves to keep his father in his life. If I can't guarantee the latter, the least I can do is make sure that boy's never in danger again."

The fine hairs on Kate's body rose in response to Stephen's determination, his desperation, to keep fighting for his client. He was a hero, as much as her brother or any of Martin's fellow officers were. Stephen's weapon was the law, and he had put his career, his very life, on the line to give a struggling family a chance.

How much harder would he fight for someone he loved? Someone he'd touched as tenderly and passionately as he had Kate—touched her so deeply, she'd fallen for him just as hard.

"Stephen." She reached for him. "I—"

"I'll have to discuss this with my supervisor," Agent Conrad said, cutting her off. "I'll need you to come with me, Mr. Creighton, until we can straighten this out."

"Stephen…" She grabbed his uninjured arm, not that she could really stop him from following.

But he did stop.

His hand came up to cover hers, squeezing her fingers reassuringly as he had so many times before. He searched her eyes, as if he knew what she needed to say. As if he still needed to hear it.

"I love you," she whispered—right there in front of her ex-husband, Marsha and the E.R. staff swarming around them. "I—"

"Mr. Creighton," the agent prodded.

"I'll be here," she promised. "As long as it takes. Don't go anywhere without me?"

Stephen swallowed. He looked toward the trauma room, then back to her.

"Mr. Creighton!" the agent demanded.

He took Stephen's bandaged arm in a persuasive grip.

"Go stay with Dillon," Stephen said. "I'll come find you when I'm done."

Kate watched him go, her heart pounding like it had the very first time she'd seen him. Except then, it had been out of fear for what he might do to her patient. Now, the fear was for herself, and the hold he had on her heart—even though it might be too late.

"You okay?" Robert wrapped an arm around her and steered her toward the elevators. A stunned Marsha followed. "Creighton's right. Spend some time with Dillon. Go see for yourself that he's okay. I'll keep an eye on the father. It looks like they have him stabilized. I'll let you know if his condition changes."

Kate nodded. She glanced over her shoulder to search for Stephen. But he was already out of sight.

"Up you go," Robert said as the elevator doors opened and she and Marsha got on. He pushed the button for the pediatric floor.

Robert was protecting her, same as always. And instead of balking, Kate let the elevator doors slide shut and leaned against her friend.

"It's going to be okay." Marsha hugged Kate to her side.

In the past Kate would have fought to stand alone. Now she let herself absorb her friend's reassurance. She didn't question Robert stepping in to watch out for Manny, or how much she needed her brother to get there. She couldn't do this without any of them. She'd take all the help she could get over the next few hours, and be grateful for it, instead of punishing herself for not being enough alone.

Stephen was still fighting for the Digarros, and so would she. Then once Dillon was settled, and Stephen was through running the table on the DEA, she had one more battle to wage.

Stephen had said he'd meet her upstairs. He hadn't promised anything more. She may have lost him for good, no matter how much she loved him and was ready to fight to believe in what they could have.

There were no guarantees. She might very well lose. But she was going to stand her ground and fight for love this time.

"How long have you been here?" Stephen asked Martin Rhodes, who was sitting on a bench outside the pediatric room Stephen had been pointed toward.

Lissa Carter rounded the corner, carrying two cups of steaming coffee. Martin took one as she sat beside him.

"Your buddy Jenkins called and told me what went down," he explained. "Once we got here, it didn't take much asking around to find out where Katie was. She's been in with the kid since we found her a little over an hour ago. How's the father?"

"Stable." Stephen rubbed a hand over his jaw. Stubble reminded him that he hadn't taken the time to shave that morning, and that morning had come and gone hours ago. "Manny's in surgery. They're repairing a collapsed lung and exploring his chest to patch up whatever's bleeding. Kate's ex seems to think he's got a good shot of pulling through."

"And then?" Martin drew the woman cuddling against him closer.

Stephen sighed, glancing beyond the APD officers guarding Dillon's closed door, through the window to where Kate sat on the edge of the boy's bed. All but one of the lights had been dimmed. Beneath the single beam, it looked like Kate was reading Dillon a story. She probably hadn't left his side once. She was right where Stephen had asked her to be, waiting for him. Trusting that he'd do the best he could for Manny, and then come find her.

I love you.

"Here." Martin handed him one of the coffees. "It's cream, no sugar, the way she likes it."

The man took a sip from the other cup, then handed it back to Lissa. He settled against the wall to wait. Whatever his sister needed next, it was clear Martin planned to be there to help her get it. At least that part of Kate's life was back to the way it always should have been.

Stephen nodded, then turned to knock softly on the closed door.

Kate glanced over her shoulder, rose from the bed when she saw him and motioned for him to come in. She'd set the book aside and smoothed the wrinkles rumpling her knit top and jeans. He set the coffee on a table near the door and stepped to the foot of the bed.

Dillon was sleeping, his car tucked under his cast-encased arm. An IV ran to his other arm from a bag of clear fluid hanging on a stand.

"How's he doing?" Stephen asked softly, looking at the boy, because looking at Kate when she was this close wasn't possible yet.

Things were still too unsettled, no matter what she'd said downstairs. She'd had a long time to rethink the challenges they'd face if they tried to make a relationship work. He'd called her a coward, when in fact she had simply been playing it safe, the same way Stephen always had.

It wasn't Kate's fault that he was out of his mind in love with her.

"Dillon's worried about his dad." Kate ruined

Stephen's plan to give her space by stepping closer.

She was so warm. After hours of danger and death and cutthroat negotiating with the people who were going to make the darkness go away for the Digarros once and for all, Stephen had grown numb to the cold that had spread inside him.

"Robert says Manny should pull through," he made himself say, through the need to kiss her, to hold her the way Martin was holding Lissa outside. Cuddling her to his side, where she'd fit perfectly. "I've told the DEA everything, and I have a written agreement that as soon as it's medically safe for them to travel, Manny and Dillon will disappear. They'll be protected. Manny will most likely have to testify at some point, once the Feds have as much of the Vargas cartel in custody as they can capture. But Dillon's going to have his father, and a home full of toys and friends and the kind of childhood he deserves."

Kate's smile was beautiful. Her tears of relief made surviving such a hellish day worth every bit of risk and legal finagling it had taken. But it was her hug, as she threw herself into his arms and held on like she'd never let go, that flooded Stephen with hope.

"Thank you," she whispered in his ear. She

was shivering, crying. She laughed softly. "I knew you could do it. I knew the Digarros could count on you, that I could count on you. I…"

She stiffened and slid away, reclaiming an inch of the distance he no longer wanted her to have. He didn't want anything separating them, while he tried to convince her to finish what she'd been about to say. What she'd said downstairs, that he hoped to God to hear again, every day, several times a day, for the rest of his life.

"You what?" His fingers curved around her waist. "You knew that you could count on me, and you…*what?*"

She hesitated for so long, he wanted to scream. But he had just enough energy left to negotiate one more big-time pay-out. The biggest deal of his life.

"I mean," she began, torturing him by wetting the corner of her mouth with her tongue. "I know we've moved fast, and I wasn't ready to hear you last night. And I know with my kind of baggage, you're probably wondering if I'm capable of committing to anything. But I… I want to be with you, on whatever terms you're comfortable with. You could move in to my place, or maybe you'd rather try living together at yours for a while. Maybe one day, if it works out, we could look into getting a new place of our own. Not that I'm trying to tie you down to anything, I'm just… I…I know I told you no yesterday, but if you'd just give me another chance… I'll do my best to convince you that I can—"

His kiss silenced her before it got worse. And he kept kissing her until she softened in his arms.

Despite the encouraging direction of her rambling explanation, he still hadn't heard what they both needed her to say. He lifted his head and waited for her eyes to open. Then he waited some more.

"And?" he asked, already feeling her response in the way her body was melting into his.

"I…I love you, Stephen." She bit the corner of her lip, then smiled. "More than I ever thought I was capable of loving anyone. I love the way you go to battle for your clients, and the way you've fought back from the disappointments in your life. The courage it took to stand up for Manny today, when he was too hurt to stand up for himself. I love you. I'll always love you. I need you to believe me. To trust me not to bail on you again. Let me try again. I can show you—"

She stopped as he shook his head. The girlish hope that had spread across her features evaporated, and she tried to pull free.

"No." He kissed her softly until she no longer struggled. "No more trying. No more giving this a chance."

She stared up at him, then nodded.

"What do you need to believe me, Stephen?" Her kiss was as tentative as her question. "Whatever it is, I trust you. Just tell me what you need."

"I need to be yours." His palm cupped her cheek. "As deeply and as permanently as I need you to be mine. Not just for now. Not once we're sure. I know it's a risk, but I don't want to play this safe. I need to be legally yours, Kate. Forever. Say that you love me enough to be mine, and the rest we'll figure out together. Marry me."

She was nodding again, silently. Then she was in his arms, and he cupped her head and pressed it to his shoulder.

"Kate?" he asked. "I'm a lawyer, and I never leave a negotiation without a verbally binding contract."

"Yes," she whispered in his ear. "Yes, I'll marry you, Stephen Creighton. And I'll love you every day for the rest of my life. Just try to get rid of me."

EPILOGUE

"WHAT ARE YOU DOING in there?" Stephen asked on the other side of the bathroom door.

"Making you wait," Kate teased. As if she wanted to be anywhere else herself but heading out the front door with her husband, to their Mediterranean cruise honeymoon. "You're awfully bossy this morning."

And she loved it.

Their civil ceremony at city hall yesterday had been brief but beautiful. Martin and Lissa had been there. Neal Cain and his wife, Jenn. Curt Jenkins had been Stephen's best man, and Marsha had stood up for Kate. She and Stephen had exchanged promises before the judge and their witnesses, but in their hearts they'd become one the moment they'd found the courage to risk loving each other.

Kate applied a final wisp of lip gloss, marveled at her reflection one last time—at the happiness radiating from her eyes and her smile—then opened the door to the gorgeous man hovering just outside.

"It's about time." Stephen pulled her into his arms and relieved her lips of their shiny coating.

He kissed her like a man deprived.

"You've had five whole minutes to yourself!" Kate swatted his shoulder. "See why I locked myself in there? We'll miss our flight at this rate."

Stephen followed her into the bedroom, staying close as she double checked her suitcase and carry-on bag. As close as Martin was sticking to Lissa these days. Lissa had scored a new job at a local bank branch, and she and her adorable girls had moved in to Kate's condominium complex. Martin spent most evenings eating at either Kate's place or Lissa's. But Kate knew she wouldn't remain in the rotation long. Not now that Martin had proposed.

Her brother would be married soon, to a wonderful woman who had helped both him and Kate see beyond their broken past. Martin was going to be okay, and so was she.

"Robert called." Stephen leaned against her chest of drawers as she zipped her suitcase. "I thanked him for the champagne. Told him we put it to good use."

"You didn't!" Kate tossed a pillow at her husband's head. Robert hadn't been at the ceremony, but an expensive bottle of bubbly had been waiting for them when they'd got in last night.

"Damn straight I did." Stephen tossed the pillow back, then tackled her to the rumpled covers she hadn't bothered tidying before she'd started to dress. "The man knew what he was doing when he sent the booze over."

The same way Robert had known what he was doing each time he'd secretly met with Martin to encourage him in his physical therapy. The same way he'd known what to do for Kate that awful day when Manny Digarro's life had hung in the balance. Now he was wishing the best for her. Kate just hoped he found someone to share his own life with, someone as perfect for him as she'd turned out to be for Stephen.

She kissed her husband and snuggled into his embrace, letting the rightness of having him close, of *wanting* him close, sink in. He settled on his side, propped his head on his hand and gazed thoughtfully at her. Despite how perfect yesterday and last night had been, despite the two-week vacation they were taking, there had been a weight on her heart all morning.

And of course Stephen had noticed.

"Do you think they're settled somewhere?" she asked, loving him more for waiting until she was ready to talk about it.

Stephen cupped her cheek.

"We'll never know where," he said. "But, yes, the Digarros are protected and starting over. They're going to be okay."

Dillon's condition would always have to be monitored and treated, but he would have access to the best care available. Stephen had made sure of it when he'd negotiated Manny's deal with the DEA. One minute, Manny had recovered enough to talk with the federal operatives himself and sign whatever paperwork Stephen had had drawn up. The next, he and Dillon had quite simply vanished from the hospital.

No chance to say goodbye. No final hug from Dillon, who'd become even more special to Kate those long days while his father was unconscious, and Dillon had needed someone to hold on to and help him believe.

"You okay?" Stephen asked.

Kate smiled.

"How could I be anything else?" She kissed him softly, then rolled to her feet and began pulling her suitcase toward the door. "That is, if you'd stop lolling around the house and take me to the airport, so I can start my honeymoon."

Stephen followed, her carry-on bag in hand. His things were already in the car.

He'd planned the whole trip, acting as excited as a kid going on his first vacation. They'd put off deciding where they were going to live. Her condo was an easy choice for now. They were both making significant changes at work— Stephen taking over more of Neal Cain's responsibilities, and Kate learning to better blend into the team of nurses she was privileged to be a part of. There was so much to figure out together, lots to still fight through, but all of it could wait.

"Let's go have some fun," he said, looping his arm through hers and leading the way outside.

For the next two weeks, all they were going to do was enjoy the sea, explore exotic ports of call and learn how to love each other more deeply than they already did. Their hearts were intertwining more every day, the way their lives had become irrevocably meshed over the well-being of one very special little boy….

Stephen loaded Kate's bags into the trunk, then pulled her into his arms.

"I love you, Nurse Rhodes," he said.

"I love you, counselor."

They'd fought the odds and found a way to trust, to be safe. To be together.

"Let's go," she said as she took her hero's hand. "I can't wait to see what happens next."

* * * * *

Melita had been expecting a chaste quick kiss of the generic variety. But this kiss with Sully was the kind that sparked a dying flame to life. The kind of kiss you can't plan for. The kind of kiss memories are built on.

The memory of her murdered lover, Nemo, came to her then and she made a starved little noise in the back of her throat. She raised her arms and threaded her fingers through Sully's hair, pulled him closer. Felt his body settle, then melt into her.

In that instant her hunger for him grew, and his for her. She pressed herself to him with more urgency, and he responded in kind.

Melita came out of her kiss-induced memory of Nemo with a start. "Wait a minute." She pushed Sully away from her. "You bastard!"

She spit two nasty words at him in Greek, then wiped his kiss from her lips.

"I thought you deserved some solid proof that I'm still in one piece." He started for the door. "The clock's ticking, honey. Come on, let's get out of here."

"That's it? You sucker me into kissing you, and that's all you have to say?"

"I'm sorry. How's that?"

He didn't sound sorry in the least. "You're—"

"Getting out of this godforsaken prison cell. Stop whining and let's go."

"Not if I was being shot at sunrise. Go. You deserve whatever you get if you walk out that door."

He turned back. "Freedom is what I'm going to get."

"A second of freedom before the guards in the hall shoot you." She jammed her hands on her hips. "And to think I was worried about you."

"If you're staying behind, it's no skin off my ass."

"Wait! What about our deal?"

"You just said you're not coming. Make up your mind."

"Have you forgotten we need a boat?"

"How could I? You keep harping on it."

"I'm not going without a boat. And those guards out there aren't going to just let you walk out of here. You need me and we need a plan."

"I already have a plan. I'm getting out of here. That's the plan."

"I should have realized that you never intended to take me with you from the very beginning. You're a liar and a coward."

Of everything she had read, there was nothing in Sully Paxton's file that hinted he was a coward, but it was the one word that seemed to register in that one-track mind of his. The look he nailed her with a second later was pure venom.

He came at her so quickly she didn't have time to get out of his way. "You know I'm not a coward."

"Prove it. Give me until dawn. I need one more night to put everything in place before we leave the island."

"You're asking me to stay in this cell one more night...and trust you?"

"Yes."

He snorted. "Yesterday you knew they were planning to harm me, but instead of doing something about it you went to bed and never gave me a second thought. Suppose tonight you do the same. By tomorrow I might damn well be in my grave."

"Okay, I screwed up. I won't do it again." Melita sucked in a ragged breath. "I can't leave this minute. Dawn, Sully. Wait until dawn." When he looked as if he was about to say no, she pleaded, "Please wait for me."

"You're asking a lot. The door's open now. I would be a fool to hang around here and trust that you'll be back."

"What you can trust is that I want off this island as badly as you do, and you're my only hope."

"I must be crazy."

"Is that a yes?"

"Dammit!" He turned his back on her. Swore twice more.

"You won't be sorry."

He turned around. "I already am. How about we seal this new deal?"

He was staring at her lips. Suddenly Melita knew what he expected. "We already sealed it."

"One more. You enjoyed it. Admit it."

"I enjoyed it because I was kissing someone else."

He laughed. "That's a good one."

"It's true. It might have been your lips, but it wasn't you I was kissing."

"If that's your excuse for wanting to kiss me, then—"

"I was kissing Nemo."

"What's a nemo?"

Melita gave Sully a look that clearly told him that he was trespassing on sacred ground. She was about to enforce it with a warning when a voice in the hall jerked them both to attention.

She bolted away from the wall. "Get back in bed. Hurry. I'll be here before dawn."

She didn't reach the door before he snagged her arm, pulled her up against him and planted a kiss on her lips that took her completely by surprise.

When he released her, he said, "If you're confused about who just kissed you, the name's Sully. I'll be here waiting at dawn. Don't be late."

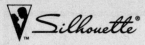

Romantic
SUSPENSE

**Sparked by Danger,
Fueled by Passion.**

Onyxx agent Sully Paxton's only chance of
survival lies in the hands of his enemy's daughter
Melita Krizova. He doesn't know he's a pawn in the
beautiful island girl's own plan for escape. Can
they survive their ruses and their fiery attraction?

*Look for the next installment in the
Spy Games miniseries,*

Sleeping with Danger

by Wendy Rosnau

Available November 2007 wherever you buy books.

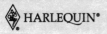

REQUEST YOUR FREE BOOKS!
2 FREE NOVELS PLUS 2 FREE GIFTS!

HARLEQUIN®

Super Romance®

Exciting, emotional, unexpected!

HSR07

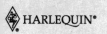

At forty, Maureen Hart suddenly finds herself juggling
men. Man #1: her six-year-old grandson, left with her
while his mother goes off to compete for a million dollars
on reality TV. Maureen is delighted, but to Man #2—
her fiancé—the little boy represents an intrusion on
their time. Then Man #3, the boy's paternal grandfather,
offers to take the child off her hands…
and maybe even sweep Maureen off her feet….

Look for

I'm Your Man

by

SUSAN CROSBY

Available November wherever you buy books.

For a sneak peek, visit
The Next Novel.com

HARLEQUIN
Romance.

New York Times bestselling author

DIANA PALMER

Handsome, eligible ranch owner Stuart York knew
Ivy Conley was too young for him, so he closed his heart
to her and sent her away—despite the fireworks between
them. Now, years later, Ivy is determined not to be
treated like a little girl anymore…but for some reason,
Stuart is always fighting her battles for her. And safe in
Stuart's arms makes Ivy feel like a woman…his woman.

Winter Roses

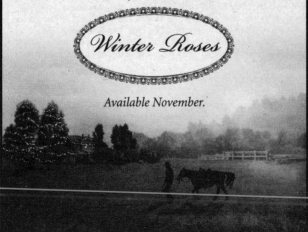

Available November.

COMING NEXT MONTH

#1452 BETTING ON SANTA • Debra Salonen
Texas Hold 'Em
When Tessa Jamison sets out to find the father of her sister's toddler, she doesn't expect to like anything about Cole Lawry, a carpenter with humble aspirations. Theirs is a secret-baby story with a twist. Because when it comes to love, the stakes are high....

#1453 A CHRISTMAS TO REMEMBER • Kay Stockham
A soldier wakes up in a hospital unable to remember anything. Before he can regain his memory, he runs into the woman he once betrayed. He can't believe that he could ever do anything to hurt someone, but there's no other explanation. Or is there?

#1454 SNOWBOUND • Janice Kay Johnson
Fiona MacPherson takes refuge from a raging blizzard in the lodge owned by John Fallon. John bought Thunder Mountain Lodge because he wanted to be by himself. Spending time with Fiona has him wondering if love might be something he wants more.

#1455 A TOWN CALLED CHRISTMAS • Carrie Alexander
A woman named Merry, a town called Christmas. Both could be just what a lonely Navy pilot who's the recipient of a Dear John letter needs. But Mike Kavanaugh isn't looking for a relationship that lasts beyond the holidays. And how can he ask that of Merry when she's expecting a little bundle in just a few months?

#1456 COMFORT AND JOY • Amy Frazier
Twins
Coming home for Christmas—to stay—is not what Gabriel Brant had in mind. Not when it means he and his twin sons have to live with his father. But Hurricane Katrina left him no choice. And now small-town do-gooder Olivia Marshall wants to heal him. Gabriel doesn't want pity. Love? That's a whole other story.

#1457 THE CHRISTMAS BABY • Eve Gaddy
The Brothers Kincaid
The Bachelor and the Baby could be the title of Brian Kincaid's life story. The perpetual playboy has just gotten custody of a baby boy. In desperation, he hires Faith McClain, a single mother of a baby girl, as his nanny. Could marriage and family life be the next chapter?